'Gina didn't ask to be born into a single parent family, and I'm giving us both the chance to try and do something about it!' he persisted.

'Okay. But can we discuss this...somewhere other than the bathroom...? Because...' Charlotte faltered.

'Because...you're really desperate for a bath? Because...you call yourself *Charlotte* now and have an over-developed prurient streak? Or maybe it's because you're terrified I might do...*this*...'

He leaned down and into her, and kissed her. No gentle, explorative kiss, but a kiss that was fiercely, urgently hungry, pinning her back against the door.

Of their own volition, her han[illegible]
and her fingers curle[illegible]
and when he flatte[illegible]
of her back and pull[illegible]
resist. She just coul[illegible]
been waiting eight y[illegible]ment to
happen, and now that [illegible] she was powerless
to do anything about it.

Cathy Williams is originally from Trinidad, but has lived in England for a number of years. She currently has a house in Warwickshire, which she shares with her husband Richard, her three daughters, Charlotte, Olivia and Emma, and their pet cat, Salem. She adores writing romantic fiction and would love one of her girls to become a writer—although at the moment she is happy enough if they do their homework and agree not to bicker with one another.

Recent titles by the same author:

KEPT BY THE SPANISH BILLIONAIRE
THE ITALIAN BOSS'S SECRETARY MISTRESS
AT THE GREEK TYCOON'S PLEASURE
AT THE GREEK TYCOON'S BIDDING

THE ITALIAN BILLIONAIRE'S SECRET LOVE-CHILD

BY

CATHY WILLIAMS

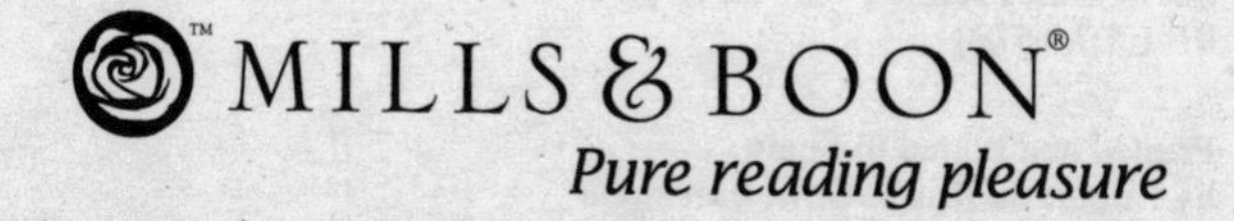

First published in Great Britain 2007
Harlequin Mills & Boon Limited,
Eton House, 18-24 Paradise Road, Richmond, Surrey TW9 1SR

ISBN-13: 978 0 263 85359 9

Set in Times Roman 10½ on 13 pt
01-1007-46791

Printed and bound in Spain
by Litografia Rosés, S.A., Barcelona

THE ITALIAN BILLIONAIRE'S SECRET LOVE-CHILD

CHAPTER ONE

JUST at this precise moment in time, life seemed very good to Riccardo di Napoli indeed. He knew, of course, that the feeling wouldn't last. Even at the young age of twenty-six, he was already keenly aware that disappointment was the shadow forever lurking round the corner, but just right now…

He had a feeling of perfect satisfaction as he briefly considered where he was. Metaphorically. The golden and only child of a couple whose name in Italy was a byword for wealth. From the moment of his birth—and probably, he thought with wry amusement, from the instant of conception—he had been lavished with everything vast sums of money could offer. He had been a child doted upon by his parents and reared to inherit the mantle of his father's massive business concerns. It was a legacy which had sat easily on his shoulders. He was bright, and to the deep and lasting approval of his father had refused to accept his birthright without earning it.

He had spent the past eight years adding credentials to his title, first from Oxford University, then Harvard, and then had come his working stint in London which had been fulfilling and hugely successful.

He had felt his first real taste of power, had noted and rather enjoyed the reluctantly won admiration from men far older than him. He had witnessed the sharpening of knives behind backs, had tasted the heady rush that comes with the making of money, and had thrilled to it.

And now here he was, poised and ready for the invigorating and cut-throat career that lay ahead of him. This little break in the Tuscan hills, as he dipped his toes into the one area of his family businesses which he had so far ignored, was proving to be as educational as it was enjoyable.

He had always been happy to drink the wine but it was interesting to get a taste for its production.

Nothing too involved, of course. His area of expertise would always be primarily in the financial arena. Still, he never suspected that the brief interruption to his pre-destined and rapid upward climb would prove as fruitful as it now was.

His eyes slid to the woman lying next to him, who was basking in the night-time warmth where the air was alive with the sounds of tiny creatures, and the sultry stirring of the trees and undergrowth in the gentle breeze.

It was too dark to make out her features, but he didn't have to. He had spent the past seven weeks almost exclusively in her company and her face and body were imprinted in his head. He would have been able to trace every small contour of her fabulous body with his eyes shut.

Oh yes. Life felt very good indeed.

As if on cue, Charlie turned onto her side and propped herself up on one elbow. She couldn't help herself. She reached out and splayed her fingers through his hair. Dark, dark hair that was worn longer than the boys she knew in England, with their silly, prissy hair-cuts and their infantile behaviour.

'I wish you weren't going tomorrow,' she repeated for the millionth time. 'I know you probably think that I'm being clingy, but it's just going to be so *lonely* here without you.'

Riccardo caught her hand and planted a kiss on the soft underside of her wrist. It made her squirm. It always did. Every time he touched her. They had just made love. Right here. With the night around them and only a blanket separating them from the prickly grass. Still she could feel her nipples hardening and every muscle in her body tensing in exquisite anticipation.

'You are insatiable,' Riccardo said huskily. He dropped his hand to her waist, running it up and under her tee-shirt, and felt the now familiar perfection of her rounded breast. He massaged it slowly, rubbing the hard nipple with his thumb.

She whimpered with gratifying eagerness, and with a smile of pleasure he pushed up the tee-shirt. The faint light from the moon showed her breasts in all their glory. True, she might be slightly built with almost no hips to speak of, but she had the breasts of a real woman. Full and rounded with big, pink nipples that were designed to be licked and teased.

As he proceeded to do now.

Charlie moaned and curled her fingers into his hair.

'No,' she gasped, not wanting the conversation to slip past, because she was so desperate to find out whether he would miss her as much as she knew she was going to miss *him.*

Riccardo ignored the protest. Actually, he was only vaguely aware that she had spoken at all. The rush of blood to his head and the fierce stirrings of his body cocooned him in a glorious bubble of pure sensation. The feel of her nipple against his tongue…the touch of her thighs as he impatiently shoved up her thin cotton skirt and pulled down her underwear…the dampness between her legs then as they obligingly parted for his questing hand…the throbbing nub of her clitoris as he roused it with his fingers. He continued to bombard her breasts with his mouth, sucking hard on first one nipple, then the next, while his own body surged to heights he couldn't remember attaining.

'Riccardo…stop…' she pleaded, making no effort to pull away from him. In fact, just the opposite. 'If you don't, I won't be able to stop myself…' She tugged his hand, and before he could return to his devastating caresses Charlie pushed him onto his back. Her near-climax was sending waves of sensation racing through her body, making her movements frantic as she did away with the clothes separating their feverish bodies. Then she slid onto him and flung her head back, eyes shut, her breasts bouncing as she controlled the rhythm of their lovemaking, until he shuddered under her just as she reached her body's nirvana.

She sagged forward, spent, and enjoyed the gentle touch of his hands on her breasts as he came down with her from his own personal peak of satisfaction.

'Have I told you that you have beautiful breasts?'

Riccardo asked, and Charlie subsided onto him with a smile.

'I believe you have. But please don't let that get in the way of repeating yourself.' She grinned and nuzzled him on his chin, loving the way the faint abrasive feel of his bristle felt against her smooth skin. She didn't think that any of the boys in her circle of university friends had *bristle*. Ever since she had become involved with Riccardo, she had blithely lumped all her male acquaintances into some indistinct category with the heading 'young and therefore immature'.

Of course, they would be, she thought guiltily. They were, after all, only eighteen. The same age as her. Not that Riccardo was aware of that little fact. She quickly shoved the thought to the back of her head and concentrated on the matter in hand—namely trying to find out how he *felt* about her. And not just the lust bit.

She clasped her fingers together under her chin and surveyed him seriously.

'Will you miss me?' she asked.

With her breasts squashed against his chest, and in the languorous aftermath of unbridled passion, Riccardo didn't find it too hard to tell her that he would.

'Not that I would call three days a lifetime,' he teased, brushing back her hair.

'I know it's not a *lifetime*, but it's a *long* time. I mean, we've been in each other's company for *weeks*. It's just going to be a little...odd, working here at the vineyard and not seeing you around and about.'

In *my* vineyard, Riccardo thought proudly, although she wasn't aware of that. As far as she was concerned, he was just bumming around, doing a bit of this and a bit of that on the production side. Since he had never in his life done any bumming around, he was quite charmed to be thought of in that light.

More realistically, there was no way he was going to give her any inkling as to what he was really all about. Gold-diggers swarmed around wealthy men like flies to a honey pot, and it was refreshing to spend his time with a woman without crazy suspicions proliferating in his head.

'It'll give you time to catch up with those friends of yours.'

'I guess it *is* only a few days,' Charlie sighed. She slid off him. 'There, you can breathe now that I'm off you.' She reached for her tee-shirt and he stopped her.

'Not yet. I like looking at you naked.'

'Just a shame most of it has to take place outdoors,' she said wistfully. 'Honestly, the amount of times I've tried to hint to Jayne and Simone that they should go spend a night somewhere so that we could have the place to ourselves…'

'A night where?'

'Oh, I don't know.' She giggled. 'Wherever it is people go to when they want to give other people space in a cramped flat.'

'Ah, *that* mystery place. I suppose if they knew of its existence they might have been more obliging.' He linked his hands behind his head, comfortable in his own nudity, and appreciated the lines of her body. The sun had turned her skin a healthy golden colour, which suited her long, streaky blonde hair and wide blue eyes. He thought, not for the first time, how much younger she looked than her twenty-four years, but then that was probably because she wore next to no make-up, which was always ageing on a woman.

'And also,' Charlie ventured tentatively, 'I'm not going to be around for much longer. I have to get back to England.'

'Yes. And that will be exciting for you. Taking up a new job, meeting new people.'

'Um, yes,' she said indistinctly, thinking of the university life looming in front of her. Two months ago, she couldn't wait to get there. Now she was dreading it after her heady summer in the sun. 'And then you'll be off as well… Do you realise you've never actually told me exactly where your next port of call is going to be?' Although, she now thought, she had told him practically everything about herself. About her dad dying when she was six, and being brought up by her mother who had worked her fingers to the bone so that her two daughters didn't have to do without. About her mother being the victim of a hit-and-run accident which had put Charlie off cars for a long time. About her sister now living in Australia, happily married and with a brand-new baby whom Charlie had never seen except on her computer.

Okay, so she had told a couple of white lies about her age, but instinct had told her that he would not have come near her if he had known that she was only a teenager. In the great scheme of things, a few white lies were easily justified.

Mostly they had been happy to be in each other's company, and that was fine.

'Who knows?' Riccardo gave a little shrug. 'The life of a wanderer…'

'And what are you going to do when you're finished wandering?'

'Settle down, get married, have six children.'

Charlie laughed, but she felt a little frisson at the thought of his kids, all with his dark hair, dark eyes and olive skin.

'You don't mean that.'

'You're right.' Riccardo thought of the life that lay ahead of him. 'I don't. At least, not yet. I have too much living to do to even go near the thought of settling down with a woman and having a family. Now, are we going to go for that drink in Lucca or not?'

'I don't know if I can be bothered.' Charlie stretched. 'Besides, I don't feel too good about using Fabio's pool. I know he and Anna are out for the evening, but I shouldn't think they'd like the thought of one of the workers flapping around on their property.'

Fabio and Anna ran part of the vast vineyards and had their own little villa and pool. Charlie, Jayne and Simone shared a flat in the nearby village and biked in every day to do their work. The arrangement worked, and Charlie didn't want to ruin it by taking advantage of her employer's absence. But Riccardo was having none of it. Youth, arrogance and a certain desire to impress the delicious woman staring up at him raced through his blood like fire. The boy who was mature beyond his years in the world of finance was right now just a young man willing to indulge an under-used wild streak.

'It's either the pool or else break into his house and use their shower...'

'Don't even say that!' But she was laughing, caught up in the energy of the moment.

'And we're here now, aren't we? In their grounds?' *Or should I say* my *grounds,* he thought realistically. 'In their grounds...in their pool...where's the difference?' Before she could say anything, he stood up and swiftly gathered up all their clothes, holding them high up and out of her reach as she scrambled to her feet, laughing.

'You're right, of course. We could always walk back to your place, but we'll have to do it wearing nothing.'

'You wouldn't dare!'

'Never challenge a man like me.' Riccardo grinned, dangling the bundle of clothes away from her frantic attempts to grab, until she subsided with a little 'humph' of mock disgruntlement.

The pool was really only a few minutes' walk through the vineyards which layered the hill in neat, orderly rows. And, once in the water, she had to admit that it was absolute bliss, beautifully cold and refreshing. And fun, touching him in the water, having him touch her. It was wicked, but how could she resist when he hoisted her to the side of the pool, lay her down with her legs dangling in the water and spread them wide apart so that he could lean at the side of the pool and taste her? A leisurely feasting with his tongue which flicked and darted, probed and squirmed. How could she resist something that felt so good?

This was what he had done to her—turned her from an ordinary, pretty teenager with ordinary, controllable relationships into a woman who was willing and eager to try anything with him. A whole new world of experiences had opened up and she had soaked them up like a sponge, loving the way he made her feel, loving *him*.

She climaxed with a long shudder of mindless ecstasy, amazed that her body could respond yet again with such involuntary urgency. Then she was content to lie there for a while before drawing her legs up and watching him as he swam like a fish up and down the lengths of the pool, before heaving himself out and then shaking off the water like a jungle animal surfacing from a river. He had utter confidence in his nakedness. He didn't seem to give a jot that she was staring at him. She was like that now with him, but at the start just the knowledge that his eyes were on her had made her want to cover her nudity with her hands. No man had seen her before without clothes, and she had shied away from his rampant masculinity, fascinated and scared at the same time.

Watching him now as he walked towards her, she wondered how he would have reacted if she had told him that she had come to him a virgin.

With horror, perhaps. Because he certainly hadn't come to her inexperienced. Anything but. Experienced men liked experienced women, was her reckoning, and besides she was supposed to be twenty-four. How many twenty-four-year-old women were totally inexperienced? He would have seen through her little white lie in an instant and that would have been the end of that.

'Ready?' Riccardo asked, running his fingers through his hair and liking the way she was eating him up with her eyes. Her amazing, big blue eyes. 'If we don't go now then we might as well head back to our respective places because I have an early start tomorrow.'

That had her on her feet in minutes. They walked hand in hand back through the vineyard to where they had left their bikes, stopping to get into their clothes when they were more or less dry.

Riccardo, thankfully, had a car. A battered old thing which he told her he had bought on his travels through the country. He was going to be using it to visit his mother the next day. She had no idea what he would do with it when he decided to push on with his travels, but he was a free spirit. She looked at him and smiled at what she saw. A man with one hand on the steering wheel, the other resting half out of the car, breeze whipping back his black hair, his classically perfect profile in frowning concentration. He drove like an Italian, as though he owned the roads.

In between their companionable silence, they made sporadic conversation until they reached Lucca, with its dramatic walls that framed the city, and which never failed to make her draw breath in appreciation.

Once parked, they went to their favourite bar which was buzzing. Riccardo slung his arm over her shoulder and drew her into him, surprised to find that he really *would* miss her over the next few days, and not just her body. She made him laugh with her amusing chatter. She was a holiday from the type of woman he usually dated.

'We should eat first,' he told her.

'Okay. Shall we go to the usual place?' Charlie, ever conscious of a bank balance that seldom reached heights that could be called truly healthy, favoured the cheap and cheerful venue.

'No, somewhere a little more upmarket, I think.'

'I can't afford anywhere expensive, Riccardo. You know that.'

'Yes, yes,' he said impatiently. 'I know. You're saving for a down payment on a house when you start your job.'

Since the only accurate part of his statement was the 'saving' bit, Charlie saw fit to change the course of the conversation just a little. 'What about you?' she protested. 'You'll need to put money aside too, if you're going to travel and see the world.' They had arrived at an expensive-looking restaurant with tables set outside. The starched white linen and bowls of flowers on the tables were a clear giveaway that her fragile bank balance would be feeling a little queasy were she to dine there. She stopped abruptly and looked up at him.

'No way.'

'You're being stubborn.'

'I'm not dressed for a place like that.' She yanked him aside so that a middle-aged couple of understated elegance could get past. 'And neither are you, for that matter!'

A lifetime of fabulous privilege had given Riccardo a keen disregard for what other people thought of him, and he shrugged.

'Honestly, Riccardo. You can be so *infuriating* at times!'

'Hmm. Does that mean you won't miss me when I'm gone?'

'Stop trying to change the subject!'

'I've never seen you hot and bothered before. Cute. Anyway, it doesn't matter what we're wearing. Who cares? Certainly not the proprietor. Competition is stiff.

He'll be very grateful for our contribution to his kitty, whatever our attire happens to be.'

Charlie gazed at him, half impressed by his easy self-confidence, half determined not to be swept out of her reality zone.

'Come on.' Riccardo cupped her elbow and guided her to the front. 'And, before you start telling me about your financial situation, this is on me.' He didn't give her time to reply. He spoke rapidly in Italian to the head waiter, so rapidly that she couldn't keep up with the translation in her head, and whatever he said must have been funny because the stiff, proper Italian actually cracked a smile.

It was the first proper restaurant Charlie had been into since she had come to Italy. The clientele was mostly over fifty, and she could feel their eyes on her, which made her self-consciously twiddle her fingers under the table until Riccardo raised his eyebrows.

To further disconcert her, he ordered wine, shooting her a quelling look just in case she interrupted.

This, he had discovered, was one of the more boring aspects of being a so-called wanderer. He was supposed to be penniless. Or at least conserving all his money for some mysterious sensible future that lurked around the fictitious corner. Despite his relief that he didn't have to be on his guard with her, there was still a part of him that would have liked to spend money on her. After all, it wasn't as though he didn't have an endless reserve of the stuff. He supposed it all came down to a pretty human desire to quite simply show off. Strange.

'You'll regret this,' Charlie said, stifling her awkwardness by very quickly downing a glass of cold, white Italian wine. 'When you're backpacking your way through some bit of Europe and you haven't got enough cash to get the train…'

'That will never be the case,' Riccardo said truthfully. Persuaded by him, she had stopped wearing a bra, and his eyes drifted to her ample breasts pushing against her tee-shirt.

He prided himself on his sophistication, but there was nothing sophisticated about what his body was doing right now. He hurriedly focused his attention on her face. Safer.

'Because?'

'Because I will…make sure I always have sufficient to get by.'

'That's fine to say, but you don't know what's around the corner.' Her friend Pete's dad had, quite suddenly, been made redundant at the age of sixty-two. They had been forced to sell the family home and move into a tiny terraced house. Life never quite worked out the way you thought it was going to.

'No, but you can hazard a pretty good guess. God, as they say, helps those who help themselves.' He lazed back in his chair and looked at her with hooded eyes. Without turning, he snapped his fingers and a waiter came charging over. Charlie marvelled at his air of command. Where on earth did he get *that* from?

'And where would you like God to help you get?' she asked, smiling, relaxed, blossoming under his languorous gaze.

'Oh, all the usual places. To a sprawling house with the sprawling lawns and the fleet of fast cars…'

'You don't really mean that, do you?'

'Why not?' Riccardo shrugged. 'When you strip away all the nuts and bolts, isn't that what everyone wants, whether they care to admit it or not?'

'I don't think so.'

'You're telling me that you wouldn't want all the things that money can buy?'

'You don't need money to enjoy life.' Charlie thought that she had never been happier than she had been over the past few weeks and money hadn't been involved. Since when had money been able to buy the beauty of the Tuscan hills with a man you loved right there by your side?

'But it enables one to eat...like this.' On cue, their starters were brought for them, a bowl of massive tiger prawns smothered in butter and garlic.

'You talk like someone who has oodles of it, Riccardo,' Charlie laughed.

'And you, *cara,* talk like an idealistic young kid who's never sampled the reality of life.'

Which abruptly reminded her that he was probably right. She needed to edit her opinions just a fraction, because really, as a woman in her mid-twenties about to strike out in a brand-new career, she would be looking towards a future that involved making money, as much as she could, so that she could enjoy all the things money could buy. Nice house with a cosy mortgage, a small house but with a bigger one on the horizon just as soon as she had settled into her imaginary job and started climbing the imaginary ladder. She nearly grimaced at the dreary prospect of it all.

'I'm trying to hang on to my inner child,' she teased.

'And so should you. I mean, you're not exactly the old man of the sea as yet. You have plenty of time to start thinking about making money.'

If only you knew. He felt a twinge of discomfort at his deception.

'I mean…' she licked her fingers before dipping them into the bowl of water with the lemon bobbing in it '…you're a free spirit. Somehow it's hard to picture you behind a desk with a mound of paperwork in front of you, and the telephone ringing and the boss yapping at you to bring him that report you should have done three days ago.'

Riccardo couldn't help it. He laughed at the comical picture she presented.

'Maybe,' he said smoothly, lowering his eyes. '*I* will be the boss yapping orders.'

'Oh no, please don't be one of those boring office people. Promise me!'

'Okay. I promise. Now, shall we enjoy this meal? The last before I head off to visit my dear mother.'

Charlie wondered about his mother. He had let slip precious little about his personal life. Oh yes, she knew what turned him on, she knew his thoughts on politics and politicians and what his favourite foods were, and all the places he had been to, but his family background was a dark area.

'Tell me about her.' Their second course was brought and, as Charlie watched the waiter deposit large white plates laden with their heavenly dishes, she missed the sudden shutter that snapped down over Riccardo's eyes. When she next looked across at him, he was back to his normal, teasing self.

'She is a typical Italian *mama*, very protective of her little boy.' That much was true. Riccardo dug into his piece of rare steak, a pleasant change from his recent diet of pasta and pizzas, and told her just enough to sate her curiosity without having to indulge in any out-and-out lying. Only when she asked where exactly his mother lived did he grow more circumspect.

Charlie knew why. There was no shame in having to admit to a parent living in reduced circumstances, but sometimes it could hit hard. Hadn't she once felt that very same thing herself? She had won an assisted scholarship to a private girls' school when she was eleven, and between the ages of eleven and sixteen, before she had left for a sixth form college, she too had sometimes found herself ashamed about her own comparative lack of money, loath to draw attention to the fact that she wasn't a member of the 'two-car, three-times-a-year-holiday-abroad' club. She tactfully and sympathetically changed the subject but it gnawed away at her, that little window into a wealth of information that would make their relationship so much deeper, that would set it on a course she was so desperate for it to follow.

Much later she was to think that love and desperation were a fatal combination.

For now, though, bitterness was an emotion with which she had never had contact. For now, she just appreciated the exquisite food and drank the exquisite wine, and wondered how she could manoeuvre the conversation back to the more fertile ground about *him*.

But he was an adept conversationalist. He didn't want to talk about himself, and so he didn't. He only had a couple more hours in her delectable company, he thought, and he wasn't going to waste it trying to dodge questions about himself. In fact, he could think of something far more profitable they could be doing…

Riccardo liked that thought. Less acceptable to him was the suspicion that he would miss more than just her willing body. Involvement with a woman, *any* woman, was not at this point in time part of his game plan.

They couldn't go back to her place. Her two friends would be there. They were 'entertaining' tonight. Riccardo had assumed that that meant having boyfriends around, but no, just an English couple they knew who were stopping by for the night. And his place was out. Which, unfortunately, just left the car. But when it came to sexual experiences, he was game for pretty much anything.

And so, he discovered, was Charlie.

Not the most comfortable place on the planet, Charlie admitted wryly to herself, but beggars couldn't be choosers, and she just wanted to touch him yet again, have him touch her once more, before he left to see his mother. She didn't even lodge a faint protest when he pulled down one of the twisting side roads and killed the engine. By now it was very late and here, away from the lights of the town, very, very dark. She was also slightly tipsy, she realised, after the better part of a bottle of some very expensive wine.

'You have some making up to do,' Riccardo murmured, wishing to hell he was driving something decent instead of this clapped-out heap of rust which he had bought because it suited the image he had wanted her to have.

'Meaning…?'

'Meaning that I satisfied you at the pool…'

'Oh, yes, so you did.' She remembered his dark head buried between her thighs and the rhythm of his tongue snaking along her most intimate places until she had bucked and moaned and reached orgasm.

They made love with the inventiveness of two people who knew each other's bodies intimately and were comfortable with the knowledge. And this time neither was left unsatisfied. In fact, Charlie thought with a sigh of contentment as they reluctantly drew apart, she seriously doubted satisfaction could get any higher.

She could have fallen asleep. In fact, she was beginning to drowse when he flipped open the car door and shifted his weight from under her.

'Nature calls,' he told her, placing a kiss on her nose. 'And then I'm going to drop you off, my little witch.'

He left the car door slightly ajar, and that was when she saw it—there, nestled in a little wad of papers which must have slipped out of his pocket in their love making. The envelope was folded in two and there, in bold type, was his mother's name and address.

Charlie picked up the envelope, suddenly very wide awake, and committed the name and address to memory. If she had had a pen and piece of paper handy she would have scribbled it down, but then that would have taken time and he wasn't going to be away for ever. She glanced nervously out of the car, made a mess of the papers and then slumped back onto the car seat where he found her a couple of minutes later.

'What's all this?' he asked.

'All what?' She yawned and sat up. 'Oh, not mine. I try and confine my bits of paper to my handbag. Must be yours. Gosh, I hope you haven't lost any more…' She began searching on the ground while he stuffed the papers back into his trouser pocket.

'Forget it. Come on. Time to go, little one.'

Charlie smiled. She believed in fate, and fate had been working overtime when it had shown her that envelope with that all-important address on it.

Because how else would she have known where he was going? And how else would she have been able to think of the one way she knew to show him that, whatever his background, he had nothing of which to be ashamed?

What better way to get to know him than by paying him a surprise visit…?

CHAPTER TWO

'BUT, Mum, I don't *like* that kind of ham! Why can't I just have some chocolate instead? *Everybody* in my class gets to bring a bar of chocolate for lunch! I'm the *only* one who brings in yucky sandwiches with yucky ham and yucky brown bread!'

'Brown bread's good for you.' Charlotte Chandler barely heard the familiar lament from her eight-year-old daughter. She was running late for work and was not open to a lengthy debate on the quality of sandwich fillings or, for that matter, the nutritional value of chocolates for lunch. 'Where's your homework, Gina?'

'In my room.'

'Well, honey, run and get it! Oh, for goodness' sake!'

She waited, tapping her heels by the front door, looking at her watch and waiting for her daughter.

Sometimes, at moments like this, she was assaulted by one of those 'what if' moments that always left her shaken.

What if, eight years ago, things had turned out differently? *What if* she hadn't decided on a stupid whim to trek in Riccardo's wake so that she could pay him a surprise visit? *What if* she had just stayed put with the two friends with whom she now had zero contact and just waited for him to return? *What if* he had loved her the way she had loved him? *What if, what if, what if?*

She had devised a method of dealing with the past, though. In her head she visualised a box, and into that box she put all those nasty, sad memories, and then she visualised herself shutting the lid of the box and sealing it down with masking tape. Most of the time, though, life was just too hectic for her to indulge her quiet regrets. And certainly, when Gina had still been a vociferous, demanding toddler, she had spent her days working flat out to meet the cost of the rent and the child minder and then flopping, exhausted, into bed at night, too tired from coping to have had much room in her head for anything.

Only now, Gina was older, and her quiet moments were no longer few and far between. It didn't seem fair that the memories that should have naturally died a death as time passed by should now start clamouring for attention.

Gina reappeared, homework in hand, already looking slightly disheveled, although it was the start of the day and she had been perfectly neat an hour before when she had got dressed for school.

Charlotte automatically reached down and smoothed some of the dark curls back into position. 'Okay. Now, you're *sure* you've got everything?'

'Sure!'

'How sure?'

'Two thousand sure.' They grinned at each other, enjoying this little game they had been playing before school since time immemorial, and then they were off.

Yet another busy Monday. A short drive to drop Gina off to school and then a far longer one for Charlotte, heading north, giving her ample time for all those unwelcome thoughts and memories to begin jostling in their box until, as she cleared the Hammersmith flyover and eased her little car onto the M4, she just sighed and allowed her mind to drift.

She knew why this was happening, of course. It was because of Ben. Because she was finally trying to get her life back on track, so to speak, by jumping back into the whole dating game instead of standing on the sidelines watching the world go by, and making excuses whenever her friends tried to encourage her to go out and meet some guys.

It was inevitable that she would be reminded of *him.* She was emerging from eight years of cold storage, for heaven's sake! *Any* guy she now saw would generate comparisons in her head.

And she was pretty sure that the comparisons were unfair, because after such a long time there was no way that she could actually remember Riccardo in any detail to speak of. She had taken no photos of him, something for which she was eternally grateful. In her head, she could still catch his smile, though, that lazy, sexy smile when he'd turned to her and reached out, and she could still remember the way her foolish heart had fluttered at the slightest contact.

She was aware of passing the Heathrow turn-off as she headed out towards the M25. She knew this route to their Midlands branch and could drive it with her eyes shut. It gave her plenty of time to think, and while she tried to make an effort to think of Ben—lovely, upwardly mobile, fantastic-catch Ben—she found herself thinking of Riccardo instead. Riccardo, who had been so shocked when she had turned up on his doorstep like an unwanted parcel that should have been delivered to another address.

She hadn't been Charlotte then. She had been Charlie. Charlie the teenager without a care in the world, madly in love, and crazy enough to have thought that the man she loved might just love her back. After all, he had *wanted* her, hadn't he? He'd told her so a million times! And how could you make love with someone with such tenderness and passion without there being just a tiny bit of love somewhere?

Finding his mother's house had been a nightmare. It had been a steaming hot day, one of those days when too much walking about made you feel slightly sick, and she had stupidly worn trousers and a tee-shirt that had clung to her like glue. Even eight years on, she could still recreate in her head all those nauseous feelings that had assaulted her as she'd tiredly travelled the distance that must have taken Riccardo, in his car and knowing the roads, no time at all.

Of course, in retrospect, she knew where the sickness had sprung from, but at the time she could remember thinking that if she didn't get to the house pretty soon then she would have to blow some of her money on a meal in one of those expensive air-conditioned restaurants as soon as she got to Florence.

Because Florence had been her destination, or rather the outskirts of Florence.

Where, exactly, she couldn't quite remember. Having committed the address to memory, she'd realised that her memory wasn't quite as obliging as she had hoped.

She had ended up spending far too much money on a mediocre meal simply because she'd been too tired to carry on trekking, and her broken Italian combined with her white-blonde hair had made her feel strangely vulnerable. Lingering over coffee, she'd realised just how much Riccardo had protected her from the open stares of Italian men. She had felt their eyes boring into her, on top of her sickness, and she had been halfway regretting the impulse to follow him.

But there had been no turning back, and besides she'd *wanted* to meet his mother, had *wanted* to prove to him that she loved him whatever his background. She hadn't cared if he didn't have any fixed plans or career path!

In the end, it was sheer luck that she landed up in the right place. After several hours, she could only remember bits of the wretched address, and she had forlornly managed to find a taxi driver with only the despairing hope that he could piece together what she recalled and somehow work out where she was supposed to go.

But, of course, she had Riccardo's name—di Napoli. And that was the key that eventually unlocked the door.

He knew the family name. In fact, knew exactly where to find the house, looked at her curiously, although she was too relieved to notice that fleeting glance.

She arrived late in the evening, and even in the fading light could see that this was not the house of a destitute woman.

'Are you sure you have the right place?' she asked the taxi driver anxiously. 'Are you sure you have the right di Napoli? I mean, there must be hundreds of them!'

A mansion faced her. It was of that distinct washed terracotta colour, but this was no simple dwelling. Portico after portico stretched along its clean main façade, and above them rows of windows and yet more doors sitting squarely behind a long balcony that extended the width of the building. And the pattern was repeated yet again. Surrounding the villa were extensive manicured lawns and trees that looked as old as time. Behind her, the taxi driver was talking rapidly in Italian, way too fast for her to understand a word he was saying, but she recognised the name Elena di Napoli, and if nothing else that was enough to make her realise that she had reached the right place. And no insignificant little place with dodgy electricity and erratic plumbing.

Charlotte felt her stomach constrict now as she remorselessly replayed the remembered scene—the old lady who'd answered the door, the old lady who had not been Riccardo's mother but one of the maids. Then his mother had arrived, then Riccardo, and from thence on her hopeful dream had turned into a nightmare.

She switched on the radio, but the distraction failed to work. Riccardo had been literally horrified, and while she had stood there, clutching her bag with all her worldly goods, stammering out that she had decided to surprise him with a visit, he had looked at her as a stranger would, with cold, black eyes, talking between her and his mother—English with her, Italian with his mother, who had the autocratic bearing of someone whom the daily inconveniences of life as most people would know it had not touched for decades. She had been tall, erect, with a long aquiline nose down which she'd stared at Charlie as though she was something the dog had chewed up and decided to spit out. Right onto her gleaming marble floor.

The minute Charlotte had managed to get Riccardo on his own, she had demanded to know how he could have lied to her, told her that he was penniless, led her to assume that he was just someone on a mission to see the world.

'I didn't *lie* to you. I allowed you to go along with your own fabrication, because things would have been rather more complicated had I not.'

Now, Charlotte switched up the volume of the music, because this particular snippet of memory was one of the most destructive. The way she had clung to him, her eyes welling up, begging him to try and explain why he was being so cold. She had been so *young*! She hadn't once, not once, clocked that he was just too accomplished to have been any ordinary person. He had been born into fabulous wealth and had the self-assurance to show for it. And even when the scales had been ripped from her eyes she had still clung to the hope that maybe, just maybe, his background wouldn't come between them. Okay, so he had lied to her about that, but she could have seen her way to forgiving him.

What a chump, she muttered to herself, driving along and frowning hard. The fog was only now beginning to lift. It was going to be one of those dank, dark days, the sort that reminded you that sunshine in late January was a rare sighting. And it was as cold to match. Her coat was flung in the back seat, and even with the heater going top whack she could still feel the iciness trying to penetrate her layers of shirt and V-necked jumper.

The trip up to the office took a little over an hour and a half, and by the time she made it there she was her usual brisk self with no outward hint that she had spent the past hour rehashing the unpleasant details of her past.

Aubrey, who owned the agency and its five branches, was as usual fulsome in his flattery and apologetic about dragging her out of the London office.

'But you're the expert on big, old houses,' he gushed.

'There's no need to lay it on with a trowel, Aubrey. It was no bother.' It was a huge bother. She had paperwork piling up on her desk, and a couple of touch-and-go sales that would require her intervention, but Aubrey had kick started her career and she owed him a great deal. Not many people would have taken her on, four months pregnant, with a stillborn university career and absolutely no experience in selling houses, never mind big ones. He had.

'How's that gorgeous daughter of yours? Any boyfriends yet? Ha, ha. Little joke.'

Charlotte grinned, nodding pleasantly at the people in the office, all of whom she knew, following Aubrey through to his separate room, fired up to get on with the viewing so that she could drive back and hopefully arrive home as early as possible. Elaine, her babysitter, was going to be there but she still enjoyed her night-time routine with Gina.

'I've told her, no boyfriends until she's through university.' Charlotte settled into the leather chair opposite him and reached forward for the particulars of the house.

'My dear girl, you mustn't let your own experiences influence you now...'

'I try not to, Aubrey, but it's difficult. Now, this house. Wow.'

'Wow indeed. We've just this minute got the particulars printed up. In fact...' he leaned back and folded his hands on his not inconsiderable stomach '...it's not even on the open market as yet.'

'And you have someone interested?'

'Several, in point of fact.'

'So it's a myth that big country houses aren't selling.' She flicked through the glossy brochure, which was presented over several pages, each with eye-wateringly tempting colour shots of various rooms and the extensive gardens. Charlotte was accustomed to these big, old properties. She asked all the relevant questions, and whether there were any sinister things wrong that would put a prospective buyer off. Many a promising sale was lost to rising damp or dry rot.

She shouldn't have made that passing remark about steering Gina away from boyfriends. She didn't want to come across as bitter, and most of the time she succeeded, but Aubrey was one of the few people who knew about her ordeal with Riccardo. He was also Gina's godfather, and so qualified to observe, not that he did that very often. Still. She stuck the brochure in her briefcase, keenly aware that he was looking at her with genuine concern and not really wanting to get into an in-depth conversation about her emotional life.

'Still seeing that young man of yours?'

Charlotte stood up and raised her eyebrows wryly.

'I'm twice your age. I'm qualified to give you little lectures about your life. Call it senior citizen advantages.' He stood up and moved round the desk and briefly put his arm around her shoulder. He was a big man. Tall and, as he enjoyed saying, a fully paid-up member of 'the fat brigade'. He dwarfed her.

'I'm taking it slowly with Ben,' Charlotte told him. 'He's a nice guy, but I'm not going to rush anything.'

'Wise girl. Right, then. I'll probably be gone by the time you finish this viewing. You have all the details in the folder. It's a woman. Phone and let me know how it goes, and let's put a date in the diary for you to come up with the little one for the weekend. Diana says it's too long since she saw you!'

'You've got a deal.'

'And feel free to bring the young man…'

'I'll have to think about that one. Maybe.' Introducing him to Aubrey and Di would be like introducing him to family, a big psychological step towards cementing their relationship onto another level. By now, they had enjoyed dinners out, the occasional theatre outing and one Sunday lunch, and she was content to keep it to that level until something kicked in and told her that the time was right to accelerate things. She had only been seeing him for three months. Why rush things along?

'Is our viewer a local person?' she asked, walking with Aubrey to the door. 'Will they be familiar with the property, or do I have to play up the location?'

'Definitely not from around here, so yes, let's hear it for the great transport links and rural setting.'

Rural being the operative word, Charlotte thought, as she left behind all vestiges of bustling provincial life and drove out into the country. It was stunning scenery. A profusion of trees raising naked branches upwards, and wintry fields stretching on either side of the winding road. In summer she imagined it would be awash with greenery.

She found herself slowing down so that she could absorb her surroundings. It really didn't matter how many big houses she walked around in London, none could compare to something in a setting like this because there was no such thing as perfect privacy in the city. You could part with millions and still have neighbours around within shouting distance. Whereas here your millions would buy you all the solitude you could ever need.

She wouldn't have minded having a look around the gardens before her viewer but that would have been an indulgence, and she was slightly relieved to find that the option was denied her because, lo and behold, there was her car randomly parked at an angle in the courtyard—a long, very expensive silver Bentley Continental, the sort that cost roughly the same price as some people's houses. Unfortunately for Charlotte, no one was in it. Nor was the woman anywhere to be seen at the front of the house. Well, there was no way she would be *inside*, not unless she had decided to embark on a little breaking and entering.

With a sigh of frustration, Charlotte walked back up to the front door and glanced around her, then she set off. She had to look at the brochure to see where the boundaries of the house lay. Frankly none were within sight, and the prospect of trekking through acres of land in search of one errant old lady with more money than sense filled her with dismay.

She was circling the back of the house, vaguely admiring the lawns and the extensive copse behind, which was all part of the package, when she heard his voice from behind her and for the first few seconds she really didn't recognise it. But only for a few seconds. Then her body froze in utter shock. Just an ordinary, polite apology that he had missed her.

Charlotte turned around and there he was: the man who still visited her in every sweet dream and every nightmare she had had over eight years. God, she had been thinking of him only this morning! Had that been some sort of dreadful, sick premonition? She blinked to dispel the reality of him standing not more than five metres away from her, and then she closed her eyes and, for the first time in her life, she blacked out.

She surfaced to find herself flat on her back with her head resting on something soft, like a cushion. There was also someone peering down at her. *Oh God.* She struggled to sit up and wriggle away from him at the same time, all the while keenly aware of the image she would be presenting—neat bob all over the place, snappy grey suit creased and soiled beyond redemption, hands covered in dirt and little chips of gravel from where she had tried to hoist herself away from him.

'Well, well, well…' Riccardo said softly. 'It's *you*, isn't it?'

'What are *you* doing here?' She sat up, gritting her teeth to ward off the sudden giddiness, and shakily got to her feet.

He hadn't changed. At least, not much. When she had occasionally imagined herself bumping into him again, she had always helpfully reconstructed him as overweight, balding and prematurely aged from the stress of all those little Italian *bambinos* his mother told her he would one day have, *with an Italian girl from his own class and not a foreigner without a penny to her name.*

But eight years had sharpened his killer looks. The black hair was short now and there were a few lines on his face but he was still devastatingly good looking. He had been kneeling next to her and he bent to brush the knees of his trousers, his expensive, hand-tailored trousers which were probably as ruined as her skirt would be but had cost ten times as much. *Tough.*

A ball of resentment welled up inside her like acid. 'I was told to expect a Mrs Dean.'

'You've changed.' He circled her like a tiger that had somehow managed to corner some interesting prey and didn't want to devour it just quite yet.

His eyes on her felt like a physical assault and she found herself cringing back. It would have to stop, she told herself. She was no longer a vulnerable eighteen-year-old girl! She was a woman with a child...*Gina.*

Fear rammed into her but she managed to keep her expression steady. She would have to get rid of him, and fast, because there was no way that she was going to allow him to find out that she had had a child by him.

No way! She had left Italy eight years ago with her life in ruins and she wasn't going to let it happen again.

'I realise you might think me unprofessional, but I'm afraid I'm going to have to let someone else show you around this house.'

'Why?'

'Isn't it obvious? We had a disastrous relationship eight years ago and that's bound to be reflected in my attitude towards you.'

'If I want this house then I'll buy it, whatever your attitude happens to be.'

'That's as may be,' Charlotte said coldly. 'But I'm not prepared to be in your company.' She reached into her bag for her mobile phone, but before she could flick it open his hand was around her wrist and he was *there*, invading every atom of her precious personal space.

'Well, that's just too bad. I've driven quite a way to get here, and I'm not about to get back into my car until I've seen this house, so you're going to get the key out of that briefcase of yours and you're going to show me around, room by tortuous room, until I'm satisfied. Got it?'

'Or else what?'

'Or else I lodge a formal complaint to your boss and make sure he understands that he's lost a potential sale, a very *big* potential sale, because of you.' Riccardo looked at her, hands stuffed into the pockets of his camel coat. His jacket, she realised, was still on the ground from where he had folded it to put under her head.

'I apologise for your jacket.' She stooped to pick it up and then stretched it out to him, making sure not to close the safe distance between them. Inside, every bit of her was shaking like a leaf.

Cornered, she stuffed the phone back into her bag and pulled out the keys to the house.

'Good girl,' Riccardo said approvingly. He had been shocked to see her, and even more shocked by his reaction which was a certain curious satisfaction, as if the wheel had come full circle, as if he had been waiting for just this moment.

Which, of course, he hadn't been. That episode in his life had been consigned to history a long time ago. She had been the casual fling who had turned, suddenly, into someone hell-bent on pinning him down. Still, it was amusing to see how much she had changed. Gone was the long, streaky hair, the fresh face, the open smile. In its place was a tailored bob and a guarded, wary expression. She was still as slender as she had been then, though, he thought as his eyes appraised the lines of her body under the business suit. As though it had been yesterday, he remembered the feel of her body under his, and was disconcerted by the impact that fleeting memory had on him.

Abruptly, he turned away, knowing that she was following him.

'I suppose you ought to know that the land extends to…there…' Charlotte pointed to various landmarks and made sure she didn't look at him. 'There's the option to buy the adjacent field, but that wouldn't be necessary as this is all a green-belt area. There's no chance that planning permission would be given for any domestic housing.'

'Estate agent. Not what I would have expected of you. But, then again, I really didn't know you very well, did I, Charlie?'

'The name is *Charlotte.*' She opened the front door, which had a series of locks, and switched off the alarm. All this was done without looking at him, although she could feel him right there next to her, sending her nervous system into panicked overdrive.

Riccardo ignored the interruption. 'No. There I was, thinking that I was dealing with a woman, and instead I was dealing with an adolescent.'

Charlotte stuck her chin up and refused to rise to the taunt. Not that she could. She hadn't *felt* like an adolescent, not when she had been around him. She had felt all woman then. But she had just been a teenager after all, as his mother had triumphantly pointed out, having rummaged in her backpack the minute Charlie had been in the shower, crying and trying to figure out what to do next. His mother had rummaged and found her passport which Charlie had brought with her rather than leave behind *just in case.*

'I point that out just in case you raise any more arguments about being the poor, deceived victim.'

'I wasn't about to raise any more arguments,' Charlotte informed him coolly. 'I was, in fact, about to point out features to the house which you might be interested in. The flooring is all original oak, as is the balustrade and banister leading up to the first floor. If you would like to follow me, there's a cellar just there…'

'Not that I intend to have a vast collection of wines stored here.'

She wanted to tell him that she really didn't give a damn what he intended to store or not store in the house, should he choose to buy it, because *he* and whatever *he* chose to do was none of her business and she could not care less.

'Oh, and that would be because…?'

'Why don't you look at me when I speak to you?'

'You were a huge mistake in my life.' She looked at him squarely in the face and thanked the Lord that he couldn't hear the wild beating of her heart. 'And why would I want to look at my past mistake?'

Riccardo forgot that over the years she had crystallised in his head as a *narrow* escape. The bottom line was that no one had ever referred to *him* as a mistake. No one. He was, frankly, outraged by her remark. Success and power accumulated rapidly over the years had built a circle of devotees around him, insulating him from the effects of personal criticism. But she was already moving on, vanishing through the door ahead of him, and he followed her with an angry scowl.

'The breakfast room.' Charlotte swept a glance round a room that was the size of most people's living areas. A huge circular table dominated the centre. To one side were two sofas, and opposite a fireplace which had retained its original Victorian tile surround. She dutifully pointed this out, aware of him behind her, releasing a force field of invisible energy that she found draining and disturbing.

'And did you manage to rectify the mistake?' Riccardo moved smoothly to stand in front of her. He wondered how he could have forgotten the blueness of her eyes and the fringing of dark eyelashes that was so dramatic against the colour of her hair.

'*This* is why I didn't think it a good idea to show you around this house,' Charlotte told him bluntly. 'Because I didn't want to be bombarded with personal stuff. There's no point to rehashing the past. It's long forgotten.' *Ha.* But to make her point, to show him that she was now a fully fledged adult, she smiled. It wasn't a warm smile but she hoped that it would prove to him that, whatever she had said, he no longer affected her.

The smile infuriated Riccardo almost as much as the 'mistake' remark. It was patronising. Yet another novel and deeply unpleasant insult to his personal pride. Thank God their relationship had ended when it had, he told himself. The woman had turned out to have the makings of a shrew in her.

'Of course it is,' Riccardo agreed, touching the Victorian tiles and giving Charlotte the distinct impression that he was only half listening to what she had said. 'If I came across as bombarding you with personal stuff then…' He glanced over his shoulder at her. 'Please accept my heartfelt apologies.'

Charlotte looked at him suspiciously. She wouldn't have put him down as the apologising sort of man, but who was to say what kind of man he was now? One thing was certain—she didn't want to antagonise him. Some instinct inside her told her that that would be a very unwise thing to do indeed. She would get through this viewing, and the best way to do it would be with a smile on her face, then she could get back to her life. Besides, maybe *she* had been at fault, bristling for no good reason and reading innuendo when there had just been curiosity.

'Sure.' She shrugged and then grinned at him reluctantly. 'I guess we're both a bit shocked to find ourselves here, facing each other after all this time.'

'So let's start again, shall we?' Dangerous curiosity began to uncurl inside him. Was she married? There was no ring, but nowadays that didn't say a hell of a lot. Maybe she was divorced. 'You look well. Life must agree with you… Are you married?'

Just at that precise moment in time, her mobile phone rang. Ben. Charlotte mouthed a 'sorry' and half turned so that she could conduct a whispered conversation, then, as she snapped shut the phone, she turned to Riccardo and said brightly, 'Not married, no. Not yet, anyway…'

There! If that didn't establish some well-defined boundaries between them, then what would?

CHAPTER THREE

RICCARDO let that ride. So the teenager had matured into a woman involved in a relationship and on the brink of marriage. It had always been her dream. Thinking back, he could remember snippets of conversation when she had confided in him that there was a little bit of her that was jealous of her sister, jealous of all that domestic stability. He could remember laughing and denigrating an institution that was based around cementing two people together, usually when they were way too young to recognise the compromises it involved, but conversations like that had only ever lasted for a short while because there had always been better things to do.

Then she had shown up on his doorstep, clutching dreams of commitment and marriage, and he had been forced to recognise that perhaps he should have paid a bit more attention to those tenuous threads of conversations that he had allowed to waft by.

He made a big mental effort to be magnanimous on her behalf, but his head was playing weird tricks on him, forcing him to remember the tantalising feel of her body writhing under him, and the way he had not been able to get enough of her. From that springboard, that slow curl of curiosity began to swell. He wondered what the man was like and felt an unwelcome jolt of jealousy.

'So…what happened to the university plans? When I found out how old you were—or should I say how *young* you were—you told me that you were on your way to university to study…what was it?'

'Land management.' Now they were entering perilous waters, and Charlotte could feel little pinpricks of perspiration breaking out all over her body.

'So what happened to the land management dreams?'

'Oh, you know…' she said vaguely. 'Dreams come and go. Look, have you seen enough of this room? Because I have a bit of a drive back home.'

'Oh yes? And home would be…?'

'Not around here!' Charlotte laughed and briskly took the lead, sweeping out of the breakfast room and heading towards the kitchen which she intended to describe in such depth that he would probably keel over in boredom. Anything to avoid him questioning her. Yes, his questions were harmless, and pretty predictable given the history they had briefly shared, but they still had her on tenterhooks.

'Now, the kitchen! As you can see, this is the perfect kitchen for entertaining!' She could hear herself teetering on the brink of a Stepford-wife impersonation. 'Double Aga, great for preparing meals for large numbers of people, and big enough to house a table for eight. The conservatory is a recent addition to the house, one of the few, but I think you'll agree that they've done an excellent job in maintaining the Victorian aspect of the house!'

'You certainly seem to be involved in what you do,' Riccardo commented dryly, bemused by her sudden departure into manic-salesperson pitch. 'Yes. This is a very…charming kitchen, although I don't intend to be doing much cooking in it.'

'No wines for the wine cellar, no food in the kitchen… what *exactly* is the purpose of the house, if you don't mind my asking?'

'Investment. I think the time is right to add a country house to my portfolio. I guarantee that in five years' time this place will have quadrupled in price.'

'In that case, is there any point in showing you around? You could get everything you need from the particulars you have in your hand.'

'Oh, I think I need to have a close up view of whether any work needs doing. It's boring, and I can't afford the time, but my assistant inconveniently caught some kind of bug over the weekend and couldn't make it.'

Charlotte looked at Riccardo's dark, sexy face and shivered at the man he had become. The winning confidence of youth had been honed into cold self-assurance. Years ago, in the aftermath of their showdown, he had coolly informed her that his future was mapped out for him, waiting for him to seize. He had obviously seized it, but it didn't appear to have made him happy because happiness wasn't etched into his features.

'Why, can't you afford the time?' she heard herself asking, and he must have detected the sarcastic edge to her voice because he directed all his frowning attention onto her.

'I'm a very busy man.'

'Oh yes. Forgot. All those big plans you had for that brilliant, golden future that had been planned for you since birth. I guess taking time out *would* be a little tricky.' Charlotte could have kicked herself for launching into a provocative personal attack, but he was just so damned *arrogant*, standing there, black eyes sweeping condescendingly over a house that was achingly beautiful and deserved to be more than just bricks and mortar bought to make money for a man who obviously didn't need it!

'Do I detect a certain amount of sarcasm in your voice? Is that part of your selling routine?'

'I apologise,' Charlotte muttered under her breath. 'Look, shall we get this over with?'

'Do I make you feel uncomfortable? Or is it just being confronted with your past mistake that's putting you on edge?'

'I'm not on edge.' She brushed past him, heading through to the main body of the house. This was not going to be a quick once-over. The place was so big that she could be doing her sales patter for much longer than she wanted, especially if he kept butting in with questions and observations.

It just showed the ugly bones of their relationship—she confused and sickeningly affected by him, and he cool as a cucumber and happy to stampede straight through her 'keep off' signs.

She virtually ran through the ground floor. She forgot about laboriously pointing out interesting features. That just took up valuable time, and she wanted to be far away from him so that she could breathe properly.

Upstairs came the bedrooms. She actually wanted to just leave him to get on with it, but she couldn't afford to have him running back to Aubrey with complaints about her performance. She loved her job and she needed it. So on they went. Guest rooms one, two, three and four, and then yet another sitting room and a study, and then the main bedroom.

Riccardo walked in and looked around the stunning oak-panelled walls. Large bay windows dominated two of the walls and through both lay extensive views of fields and woodland. He noticed that she hadn't followed him in but that she had remained hovering by the door, clutching her brochure.

Impatience mingled with irritation. So, yes, she had admitted that she had made a mistake with him, but did she have to take her aversion to such obvious lengths? She clearly couldn't wait until they were outside and she could speed off in the opposite direction. He supposed it said something that she could still be affected by his presence after all this time, but he wasn't idiot enough to think that that something was remotely flattering. Anyone bitten by a snake would probably shy away from too many future personal encounters with the species.

Accustomed to the adulation of women, Riccardo gritted his teeth and did what he had come to do. He peered at the woodwork, looked at the window frames, tried to work out what fundamental work would be needed if he bought the place. Behind him, he could sense her waiting, keen to leave, probably looking at her watch.

'There's another floor,' Charlotte said, as soon as he turned around. 'It's been used as a suite of guest rooms, but it could be turned into pretty much anything. Would you like to have a look?'

'No. I'd like to give that a miss, because I really don't object to tossing a couple of million at a property having only seen a fraction of it. I'm really getting a little impatient with your wounded-party act, Charlie.'

'Charlotte,' she said quickly. 'I'm not that girl you knew any more!'

Riccardo took a couple of steps towards her, and Charlotte swallowed hard but stood her ground until he was towering over her, face grim, ebony brows winged into a dark frown. Everything about him terrified her. Life for the past eight years seemed to have been a pleasant, trouble-free walk in the park compared to just this one single moment in time.

'No, you're not. You're a woman about to be married who clearly can't stand the sight of me and isn't mature enough to conceal it.'

'Can you blame me?' Charlotte said in a high, accusing voice. Logic and common sense flew through the window, and in its place was a red mist of remembered hurt, misery and resentment. 'You led me on…'

'I promised *nothing*!'

'You slept with me.'

'I wasn't the first!'

'Yes, you damned well were!' She had never told him. Now it was out, and he stared at her in shocked silence.

'You couldn't have been. I would have known.'

'How?' Charlotte demanded, her cheeks burning. 'How would you have *known*?'

'There was no…there were no signs…'

'Oh, please! I was eighteen and you swept me off my silly feet.'

Would he have slept with her if he had known that she was a virgin? Riccardo asked himself. No. No, he wouldn't have, because his keen antennae would have alerted him to the inherent problems. He also would have started asking a few more questions about her age because twenty-four-year-old virgins, in his experience, were pretty thin on the ground. He surfaced to find that she was still attacking him, fuelled by eight years of blistering resentment.

'No, you don't!' he cut in harshly. 'If I had known that you were a virgin, whether you were eighteen, twenty-four or fifty-six, I wouldn't have slept with you!'

'Because?' She heard herself ask the question with dismay and knew that she should have listened to her head and not allowed her emotions to run wild.

'Because you would have been vulnerable!'

'And all you wanted was sex,' she whispered bitterly.

Riccardo swept his fingers through his hair and flushed. 'That is *not* what it was all about!'

'No? And that would be why you stood up for me when your mother started ranting about my unsuitability?'

Riccardo released a long, audible hiss of frustration. Those big, accusing blue eyes were making him feel like a cad and, damn it, he didn't deserve that!

'My mother wanted…'

'Oh, yes! I know what your mother wanted—a good Italian girl for you! Someone with all the right connections! She made herself perfectly clear on the subject. In fact, she mentioned a certain *Isabella*. Perfect credentials! Did she make it to the altar after all?'

'No one made it to the altar,' Riccardo muttered, glowering at her. Her face was suffused with angry colour. She might have changed the haircut, and swapped her tee-shirts and short skirts for a business suit, but look past that and there was still the same girl underneath.

'You're right,' he said heavily. 'I should have stuck up for you a bit more.'

'*A bit more?* You didn't stick up for me at *all*! In fact, if my memory serves me, you were horrified that I'd landed on your doorstep!'

'It was unexpected.'

'An unexpected and unpleasant surprise,' Charlotte amended, recalling it as if it had all happened the day before. 'Especially to a young, vulnerable kid who thought that the first man she slept with might just turn out to be somebody who cared.'

'And I was twenty-six who thought he had been having a pleasant fling with a twenty-four-year-old woman. A twenty-six-year-old with his career stretching in front of him and no thoughts of marriage on his mind!'

'I never said that I wanted to *marry* you!' But she had wanted a relationship, not just a meeting of bodies until they went their separate ways. And where else had that been heading but down an aisle somewhere along the way? Why kid herself? She shifted uneasily on her feet and tried not to see his point of view, but like it or not it still crawled under her skin and she reluctantly had to admit that he had just run scared, confronted by someone he thought wanted to tie him down. The age thing had probably been the final straw.

And now there was Gina.

'And you have to understand that my mother is a traditionalist. A young, blonde English girl appearing on her doorstep would have been her worst nightmare.'

Charlotte was finding it somewhat harder to picture his mother as a kindly old lady who just happened to have been caught in a time warp.

'Well, now that we have got that out of the way, maybe we could finish this tour of the house,' she said tightly. They said that confession was good for the soul but, having spilt her guts, she just felt confused.

By the time they were back in the hallway, Charlotte was wrung out, even though nothing further had been said between them. She had said all the right things about the house and he had asked all the expected questions.

It was already dark And gloomy outside, even though it was still just mid-afternoon, and it was cold.

'So…' She looked at him when they finally made it outside, already feeling safer with her little car next to her. 'If you're interested, then you can get in touch with Aubrey James at our Henley office and he can take it from there.' His face was all dark angles, and she shivered and wrapped her coat tighter around her.

'Why not you?'

'I beg your pardon?'

'Wouldn't it be more logical to get in touch with you, considering you were the one to show me around the house?'

'No!' She clicked her remote and yanked open the door of her car. 'I mean, no, it wouldn't, because I don't actually work at Aubrey's branch.'

'Well, where *do* you work?'

'In London,' Charlotte admitted reluctantly. 'But I have a good track record with selling grand old houses, and Aubrey likes to think that that makes me some kind of expert.'

'Handy when the boss gives his employee special favours.' Riccardo wondered whether this was the fiancé, to whom she was as good as married, bar the details. 'Is this the soon-to-be bridegroom?'

'The…? Oh.' She remembered her passing remark about Ben, that distance-creating manoeuvre that hadn't worked. Poor Ben. What would he think if he knew that he had featured as a likely fiancé? She grinned, her first genuine smile of real amusement. 'No. No, Aubrey isn't any bridegroom in the making. In fact, he's very happily married and twice my age, height and girth. Father figure sooner than bridegroom, I would say.'

Riccardo watched that smile, just the shadow of it, in the swiftly descending gloom and drew in his breath sharply. He'd remembered that, kept the image of it somewhere in his head, even when time had moved on. Curious. And unsettling.

'So, who *is* the lucky man?' he asked lightly, and Charlotte couldn't find a reason not to name a name. It would have been odd if she had tried to withhold the information, she reasoned, because women on the verge of marriage were supposed to be happy and proud of the fact.

'Ben.'

'And Ben is…?'

'Oh, the usual. A man. Couple of arms, couple of legs, head.'

Riccardo gave a rich, throaty chuckle of amusement, and in the darkness Charlotte blushed and remembered that she needed to be on her way, far from the man standing in front of her, who it seemed still had the ability to get her hot and bothered. She had to get back to her daughter.

Their daughter, her mind flung back at her.

'And what does the arms, legs and head do?'

'Nothing! I really must be off now. I don't want to end up driving in the dark. Especially as it's such a long drive back to London.'

'Surely if your boss has such a high opinion of you he would get you somewhere to stay for the night, save you the drive down?'

'Oh, no, I can't stay here!' No sooner were the words out than she wanted to swallow them back down. 'I mean… I mean…'

'I know what you mean,' Riccardo interrupted her brusquely. 'Young love. I guess the man whose job is *nothing* is waiting for you somewhere in London with a spread in the oven and candles on the table. You have to be careful, you know.'

'Careful? Careful of what?' It was difficult keeping up with him, especially when his conclusions were so far off-target—a fact for which she was extremely grateful.

'Men who kick off a relationship by making sure you're chained to them. It might be flattering to start with, but no one enjoys being a captive.'

'I don't know what you're talking about,' Charlotte said waspishly. It particularly made no sense, considering she and Ben were still in a 'maybe, maybe not' situation. Nevertheless, in view of the fact that she had been creative with the truth, Charlotte felt morally obliged to defend his good name. 'I'm not a captive, for goodness' sake.'

'Then why the panic?'

'I really have to go.'

'I'm heading down to London myself. I could always follow you, make sure you get to your house safely, for old times' sake. These roads can be treacherous in winter.'

'No!'

Riccardo put up both his hands in mock surrender. His curiosity was now seriously piqued.

'I'm fine to drive back unescorted, thank you very much. I've done longer trips.'

'And travelled back to London on the same day? When it's getting dark? In that tiny little sewing-machine of yours?'

'It's very reliable!'

'But not exactly equipped for long-distance driving.'

'I don't believe in great, big gas-guzzlers.' She looked meaningfully at the great, big gas-guzzler parked behind him.

'Yet in the event of an accident, on a dark road in the middle of winter, you might find yourself regretting that you cared more about the planet than your own safety. Is that a company car? If it is, then I think I shall have a word with that boss of yours, find out what he thinks he's playing at, sending you all over the country in something that's only fit for city driving…'

'Don't you dare!'

'You know, you should never mention my name and the word "dare" in the same breath...'

Charlotte wondered whether he was joking. It was hard to tell, because the light was so poor and she couldn't read the expression on his face, but still a little whisper of danger fluttered along her spine.

'Why are you so jittery?' he asked curiously. Riccardo knew that this was a conversation that was going nowhere. She would drive off and so would he, and later he would just think of their meeting as one of life's strange coincidences. But for the moment he had the strangest need to carry on talking to her. 'I mean, it's soon going to be dark.' He shrugged, a casual, elegant movement that she remembered well. 'So where's the rush? Why don't I take you out to dinner? You can continue ranting at me, and then when you're through we can do some civilised catching up.' Riccardo liked his use of the word 'civilised'. It made him sound ferociously controlled, and papered over the alarming suspicion that for the first time in years he was not responding to a situation with his head. His head was definitely not telling him to ask out a woman who was treating him like an infectious disease.

'Sorry, can't.' She opened her car door and flung her bag and briefcase in the passenger seat, then she clambered in. But before she could slam the door behind her he was there, propping it open with one lean, brown hand, and bending down to stare at her. And unfortunately for her, with the car light on, there was no way she could conceal the agitation on her face. She knew how she looked: red faced and as guilty as hell. Naturally he wouldn't know *why* she looked guilty, but he would be curious, and even after all these long years she knew him well enough to realise that there was one trait he possessed which would surely not have changed—tenacity. He had always found pursuit in the face of a challenge very invigorating.

'My boyfriend. Well, fiancé…' She sat on her hands and crossed her fingers.

'Ben with the nothing job.'

'Actually, he's a chartered surveyor. And—and you were right. He's actually waiting for me. He's cooked me a meal. He always does that whenever I happen to be on one of these jobs…you know…when I won't be getting back until late. He's a great cook. Loves it.'

Riccardo frowned heavily, and Charlotte, feeling a lot more comfortable now that she had established an alibi for her red face, laughed lightly and started her engine. 'Yes, I know you'd probably disapprove. I guess, coming from that traditional Italian family of yours, you probably think men who cook are wimps, but there you go! Ben is a fantastic cook, and there's nothing he enjoys more than looking after me!'

'He must have a very flexible working environment,' Riccardo drawled. 'If he can find the time to hurry home and indulge his love of cooking whenever you happen to be on the road after five thirty.'

How had she known that he would manage to shape his remark into a veiled insult? That great, big fat ego of his probably couldn't stand the thought that she had bagged herself the perfect man.

She sighed a sigh of resounding pity for him. 'You know, all that paper chasing…'

'Paper chasing?'

'*Money*, Riccardo. Selling your soul for pots of gold…sacrificing everything for a big bank balance… Well, that's the domain of the dinosaur! It's the twenty-first century, and these days people are finally waking up to the fact that there are more important things in life than foreign holidays and big cars! And Ben is a twenty-first-century man. He arranges his time so that he can really fit in the things he enjoys doing!'

'Cooking…and what else? Cleaning, ironing and needlework?'

Charlotte chose to ignore his predictable sarcasm. 'Ha ha, Riccardo. You might think you enjoy working twenty hours a day so that you can rake in more and more money, and buy beautiful old houses like that one as *investments*, but as far as I'm concerned Ben has discovered the *real* secret of happiness. He's said goodbye to *greed* and hello to a more spiritual and *fulfilling* life.'

'And you're content with all this tree-hugging stuff?' Riccardo laughed shortly. 'I don't believe it!' He worked damned hard, he told himself, and he enjoyed it. Not because of the money. Hell, it wasn't as though he *needed* to make any more of the stuff! He enjoyed it because it fired his blood, made him feel alive.

'Well, I don't actually care *what* you believe. Now, if you don't mind, I want to go. To that delicious hot meal waiting for me. And a man who knows that there's more to life than a fat bank balance!'

Driving away, Charlotte had the feeling that she had won the battle, and the war as well. She had established herself as a thoroughly modern woman who had moved on with her life and now had her priorities firmly in place.

She even found herself humming along to the radio station until that kick of triumph started wearing off, at which point she realised that she had won nothing at all.

Sure, in *his* eyes, she had succeeded in fabricating the image of a woman in control, the complete opposite, in fact, of the dithering kid he had demolished eight years previously.

But, in reality, there was no fabulous fiancé rustling up mouth-watering dishes for her every evening. She didn't even know if Ben could boil an egg! They had eaten out whenever they had met. And, yes, she really *did* disapprove of a man whose *raison d'être* was money. But she worked her socks off to maintain a decent life-style for herself and Gina, so where was that twenty-first-century road she had proudly declared herself going down? Somewhere on a very distant horizon!

And should she have told him about Gina? The thought filled her with horror. Who knew what he would do? The worst case scenario filled her head like suffocating poisonous fumes—he would go ballistic and then his Italian side would kick in and he would take his daughter. He would use all that fabulous wealth at his disposal to guarantee Gina at his side, whatever the cost. She shuddered.

In the morning, she would telephone Aubrey to let him know how the viewing had gone, and in passing she would mention the identity of the prospective buyer and swear him to silence on the subject of his goddaughter. Just in case Riccardo decided to ask any questions about her. She very much doubted that he would, but just in case…

It was always better to be safe rather than sorry.

CHAPTER FOUR

CHARLOTTE propped her chin in her hand and looked intently at Ben, whose niceness over the past two weeks had been teetering precariously on the brink of boring. She was determined, however, not to find him boring, and in fact at moments like this, when her mind was beginning to glaze over as he enthused over some particularly tedious event at work, Robinson, Hathaway & Sons, she reminded herself that niceness was the stuff of all good, successful relationships. All that 'frisson' business was much overrated, as she had discovered to her cost. And she and Ben were beginning to have a relationship. They hadn't slept together but they had shared a few lingering kisses, which he had attempted to progress. But she had firmly told him it was simply too soon and he had gallantly respected her decision.

She had breathed more than one sigh of relief that Riccardo, having appeared from thin air to throw her into panicked disarray, had also disappeared similarly quickly. He had spoken to Aubrey, who had been fully briefed on fending off any questions about her, had told him that he would go away to think things over in connection with the house, and that had been the last the agency had seen of him.

The fact that his appearance had reignited a maelstrom of memories was just something she knew she would have to deal with. And she was, by really focusing on Ben and harnessing her stubborn mind with frequent, stern lectures.

She snapped out of her daydream to find that Ben was waiting for her to say something. *What? What? What on earth had he been talking about?*

'Yes,' she said automatically, which produced a smile of pleasure.

'Great. I know some women don't like being the first on the dance floor, but you're a game gal. My lady...this dance!'

Charlotte watched in horror as she realised what she had agreed to. They were in a jazz club, one which was currently sporting an empty dance floor, despite the fact that the music was good and the tables arranged around the circumference were brimming with people. And she was about to make a complete fool of herself by strutting her stuff with Ben.

'Sorry!' She smiled brightly and ignored the outstretched hand. 'Misheard. Thought you asked if I'd ever been to France!'

Ben had started doing a little wiggle in front of the table, hand still beckoning. Lord, why? Even though he was not in full flow, Charlotte could see that he would be one of life's enthusiastic dancers as opposed to one with rhythm.

Now he was threatening to move round the table and

hoist her to her feet and she stood up, glancing with deep embarrassment around her, and took to the dance floor.

'You should have warned me about this!' she yelled into his ear. 'I would have prepared myself!'

'How?'

'By drinking twelve bottles of wine beforehand!'

'You're doing fine!'

She swore that the wretched live band stretched the short number out for as long as possible just for the cabaret spectacle, and even more mortifying was the round of applause that greeted them at the end of the number. And she had been right about Ben. He flung himself around the dance floor like someone hopping on red-hot bricks and, having broken the ice, didn't seem inclined to do the decent thing and scuttle back to the table.

But at least the dance floor was filling out the way it did when two people had broken the ice by making perfect fools of themselves. And it was a slow number, so no more kangaroo hops, at least for the moment. When he wrapped her in his arms, Charlotte forced her body to relax against his and was just beginning to believe that really, yes, she was feeling some kind of physical link between them, when she felt a tap on her shoulder. She raised her head and there he was, staring at her with something close to amusement, and she felt her stomach clench into a knot of pure horror.

What on earth was Riccardo doing in a jazz club in the centre of London? Didn't he have empires to run and universes to conquer? And how was it that, having been absent from her life for the past eight years, he had now been seen twice in the space of a fortnight?

'May I?' He was looking at Ben with a pleasant smile and, poor innocent that he was, Ben was responding with a warm smile back. Couldn't he see that the man was a viper? 'I'm an old friend.'

Charlotte felt Riccardo's hand on her elbow and opened her mouth to stage a protest, only belatedly remembering that she and Ben were supposed to be engaged. What if Riccardo decided to offer his heartfelt congratulations to the happy couple? She plastered a smile on her face and stood between both men, her back to Riccardo, physically keeping them as far apart as she could to prevent any unfortunate conversations taking place.

'You sit!' she shouted to Ben over the music. 'You can get me something to drink—one of those cocktails!'

'Obedient little puppy, isn't he?' Riccardo said, swooping her into a twirl and then pulling her back into him so that their bodies met with way too much force for her liking. Like sleight of hand, he had managed to manoeuvre them into the corner, where the music didn't seem quite as loud so Charlotte didn't have to yell to reply.

'What are you doing here?'

'Do I read disapproval in that question? As far as I am aware, I don't need a special pass from you to get into a jazz club in London. If you remember, I happen to like jazz very much.'

Charlotte was remembering lots of things, and his love of jazz music was the least disconcerting of her memories. She remembered dancing with him out in the open to some tinny music from the speakers on her radio, she remembered the feel of his body pressing against her and the way she had laughed, throwing her head back, looking forward to where all that sexy dancing was going to go later.

'I saw you on the dance floor with the fiancé,' he murmured into her ear. 'Very brave of you.'

'Yes, well, Ben is adventurous like that,' Charlotte said coolly. Every time she tried to inch away from him, he pulled her gently back, his hand placed firmly in the small of her back.

'The man is a paragon.'

'Who are you here with?' Charlotte asked in an attempt to steer the conversation away from her paragon non-fiancé. He would be there with *someone*, or more probably several people, all of them high profile and ultra-glamorous. Riccardo was not a man to indulge his love of jazz by coming to a club on his own.

'A very attractive blonde, as a matter of fact.'

Charlotte felt a jab of pain. 'And you've left the poor woman on her own, to dance with someone who doesn't want to dance with you?'

She felt his hand tighten fractionally, and that felt good because she knew that her remark had got to him. The great Riccardo di Napoli wouldn't like being told that a woman didn't want his company. The great Riccardo di Napoli, with his attractive blonde who was probably sulking in the corner at being left on her own. Well, Charlotte only hoped that it would point the poor thing in the right direction, namely the nearest door through which she could exit as fast as she could if she knew what was good for her.

'He's exactly as I imagined from what you said,' Riccardo drawled. Out of the corner of his eye, he could see Lucinda focus on them, and even in the subdued mood lighting he could detect her frown of displeasure. She was getting demanding and that, didn't sit well with him. He would have to deal with that, but later. Right now, all he could think of was the woman he was holding, the one who wanted to get away. He moved them expertly around, so that his back was to Lucinda's pouting face. 'Looks like a sensitive guy.'

'I'm not going to have this conversation with you.'

'You used to believe in fate. Do you remember?'

'That was then and this is now, Riccardo.' So *that* was his date! Hard to miss, Charlotte thought sourly, considering her height. Six feet at least, with those lethal-weapon stilettos, and hair down to her waist. The sort of woman accustomed to turning heads, several of which were obeying the primitive laws of attraction and swivelling predictably in her direction. Charlotte wished she had worn heels now, if only because they were brilliant at bolstering confidence. But she wore heels every day to work, sensible pumps, and on weekends she liked reverting to flats.

Unfortunately she felt at a depressing disadvantage as she looked up at Riccardo's lean, dark face and met black eyes staring right back at her.

'I gave up believing in fate roughly eight years ago, as a matter of fact. I thought that fate had prompted me on that journey to your house and I couldn't have been more wrong. These days I prefer to make decisions a little more rationally.'

'So you don't think fate had a hand in bringing us together at this point in time?'

Was he flirting with her? Voicing some kind of academic question? Playing with her like a cat plays with a mouse, just to see what it will do? She stiffened.

'Only if fate has a sick sense of humour.'

The music came to an abrupt halt and she quickly pulled away as the leggy blonde Lucinda weaved a dramatic path through the little crowd on the dance floor.

'I think your date's calling, Riccardo!' Charlotte sniggered. 'And she doesn't look too impressed. I should watch out if I were you. Looks like she can pull a mean punch.'

There was nothing more satisfying than getting the last word, she decided as she headed back to Ben, who had obediently got her the cocktail which she no longer wanted.

Before he could say a word, she sat down and leaned closely towards him.

'Small problem,' she said as casually as she could. 'It's really about that man.'

'The man who twirled you across the dance floor? He's very good on his feet, isn't he? I always think that's the problem with Englishmen. They can be a bit stiff when it comes to dancing. Bit like me.'

'You're great, Ben.' She had visions of Riccardo swooping over with the blonde draped on his arm, asking the ridiculous but obvious question 'so when is the big day?' She gulped down a generous mouthful of her Up Against The Wall cocktail. 'But that man is Gina's father…'

Ben's mouth dropped open, and into the surprised silence Charlotte quickly gave him the bare bones of her little white lie.

'I'm truly sorry, Ben. I know I shouldn't have involved you in this, but I honestly didn't know what to do. He doesn't know about Gina and I can't risk him finding out, and…and…'

Ben looked at her shrewdly. 'So we're engaged. Well. Hasn't he noticed that you're not wearing a ring?'

Charlotte shrugged and looked at her slim, smooth ringless fingers. 'And there's something else,' she admitted sheepishly. 'He's… Well, one of these arrogant types, and I sort of implied that you were completely the opposite… You know, loves cooking and listening to music, you know what I mean…'

Ben made a face. 'I can't cook to save my life.' He grinned. 'So we're not engaged,' he said, reading the situation. 'But we're good friends, and if pretending is what you want then we might as well make a good job of it.'

'We probably won't have to!' Charlotte said but when she saw Ben raise his eyebrows and glance over her shoulder she knew that pretending was precisely what they were going to have to do. She looked around to find Riccardo and his Amazon model girlfriend approaching their table. Together they made a striking couple, and as Charlotte had predicted Lucinda was hanging onto his arm, making sure that any greedy female knew that this was her man. Poor, misguided woman, Charlotte thought.

'Riccardo!' She was aware of Ben playing his little game of ownership by placing his hand possessively over hers. 'You're still here! And you must be Lucinda?' She smiled broadly and then, wide-eyed and the picture of innocence said, 'Riccardo couldn't stop talking about you when we were dancing!' Oh yes, that met with the predictable response. Delight in her, tight-lipped disapproval in him. 'I gather you two are in a very serious relationship. Tell me, Riccardo, are congratulations in order?' It was all she could do not to burst out laughing as he tried to back out of the corner into which he had been pushed. He deserved it. Any man who made it his business to string women along deserved to occasionally face the consequences of his actions.

If looks could kill, Charlotte thought that she would have been six feet under by now. She was playing with fire but, with her so-called fiancé at her side, was safe in the knowledge that there was no way she could be burnt.

'Because they are for us!' Ben piped up while Riccardo continued to seethe. 'I've found the perfect woman!' He leant towards Charlotte and playfully rumpled her hair, which didn't strike her as the most romantic of gestures but it worked, judging from the brooding frown on Riccardo's face.

'And Charlie has spoken a lot about *you*,' Riccardo said smoothly, detaching Lucinda from his arm so that they could sit. He had used her nickname deliberately, knowing that it would resurrect memories she wanted to exorcise. If she wanted to play games with him, then who was he not to oblige?

'Yes, I have!' Charlotte gritted her teeth at the familiar use of 'Charlie' and gave Ben a wide, Tinseltown smile. 'I've told him what a gem you are! Always there, making sure I eat well and look after myself.' She looked at Lucinda. Lord, but the woman was a beauty. Right now a vaguely bored looking beauty, but she even managed to pull off bored without losing her glamour. Something about the way she tossed that mane of hair and let her lips fall into a natural pout. 'Guess you find that yourself…?' She flashed a woman-to-woman smile at her and felt Riccardo's glare.

Lucinda gave her a blank look. 'Well, Ric doesn't cook much, if you know what I mean…'

'No?'

'No,' Riccardo said flatly. 'Why cook when someone else can do it so much better?'

'I guess it depends on how much money you have to toss around in restaurants.'

'Oh, I also have my own personal chef.'

'And so do I,' Charlotte returned snidely.

'Bossy lady, isn't she?' Riccardo said to Ben, who had been following their back and forth conversation with interest. 'Like being called someone's "personal chef", do you?'

Charlotte felt a flare of anger and swallowed it back. *Bossy lady!* Coming from the king of arrogance, that was rich! She stood up, not giving Ben time to try and think of something clever to say. He was no match for Riccardo and she wasn't going to sit back and watch him demolished.

'Aubrey says you haven't been in touch about the house,' she said, changing the subject. 'Have you found a better investment somewhere else?'

'It's still under consideration.' Riccardo looked her straight in the eyes. Still as sexy as hell, he thought. Lucinda might be beautiful, but Charlotte was sharp and he liked that. In fact, he had forgotten just how much of a turn-on it was. His dark eyes slid across to where Ben was hurriedly downing the remains of his drink and standing up. The man was either firmly under her thumb, a complete bore with no mind of his own, or the perfect soulmate in a passionless love match, because he wasn't reading anything in their body language.

He shifted so that he could look at them both, and was invigorated by the thought that *he* seemed to rouse her passion a hell of a lot more than her fiancé. Her fiancé who was obviously tight with money, judging from her lack of ring. Of course, her passion might not be of the hop-into-bed variety, but there was a fine line between the passion of anger and the passion of lust. Two sides of the same coin, he thought. He felt the sudden pull of forbidden attraction, and for a few seconds, staring at her, there was no club around them, no fiancé, no Lucinda. He was back in Italy, his body on fire, his head filled with thoughts of when, how and where he was going to bed her.

'And I'll be in touch.'

'What?' Charlotte said sharply.

'About the house. I'll be in touch.'

'Well, you have Aubrey's number.' She turned away, leaving a goggle-eyed Lucinda suddenly very much interested in conversations about houses.

'He'll hate that,' she confided triumphantly to Ben as soon as they were outside, settling themselves into the back of a black cab. 'Some woman with stars in her eyes at the thought of houses and domesticity.' She was so involved in savouring her small bittersweet victory that she missed Ben's thoughtful expression as he watched her, as she leaned forward slightly, her eyes fixed on a distant horizon.

'Least of all a woman who doesn't conform to the well-connected Italian *signorina* he's signed up for. Poor Lucinda. All the looks in the world couldn't buy her an entry into that rarefied Italian world of his.'

It was half an hour before she found that the taxi had stopped outside her house, and only then did she realise that she had been boring the pants off Ben for the entire journey. But the babysitter was waiting inside and there was just no time for lengthy apologies. Just for a grateful peck on the cheek that he had rescued her from a hole that might just have caved in around her.

She hadn't expected him to get in touch with Aubrey. There was no reason for him to buy his big investment house in any particular place, and he would take his time, making sure that he didn't throw good money behind something that wasn't going to reap him the maximum profit.

Anyway, he would be too busy trying to disentangle himself from the lovely Lucinda, just as he had disentangled himself from *her* eight years ago when she had foolishly believed that they'd been more than just a passing fling.

So on the Saturday morning, half an hour after she had returned from dropping Gina to play with one of her friends from school who lived a couple of streets away, Charlotte thought nothing when the doorbell went. She lived in a semi on a pretty, busy side street which looked deceptively peaceful because someone, years ago, had thought to plant trees here and there along the pavements. She was accustomed to people knocking on the door trying to sell her anything, from window cleaning to one-to-one power-yoga tuition.

Dressed in faded dungarees, hair scraped back with an Alice band and with her furniture polish in one hand—because she'd been going to utilise her Gina-free time by getting down and dirty with her cleaning stuff—she pulled open the front door, and froze.

'You're going to ask me what I'm doing here. I know.' Riccardo glanced behind her to the white, white walls, the glimpse of abstract paintings, the bare pine floorboards, then he returned his attention to her shocked face. All her colour had drained away and her eyes looked enormous. He could see her think about closing the door on him, but she must have realised that the gesture would have been a futile one because he knew where she lived and he would come back. Also, he had managed to inveigle a position in the doorway which would have made any door slamming pretty difficult.

'Go away,' Charlotte said shakily. 'You can't just…just *show up* on my doorstep like this! If you want to discuss the house, you have to talk to Aubrey. How did you get my address anyway? How do you know where I live? Did Aubrey tell you?'

'No. Are you going to invite me in?'

Charlotte considered her options quickly. She either forced him to go, somehow managed to slam the door in his face, which would certainly involve a struggle, and he would return. She knew he would. Or she stayed on her doorstep holding forth and thereby risking Gina appearing unexpectedly. Or she politely invited him in, listened to what he had to say, and then dispatched him without fuss. No contest—option three. She pulled open the door and stepped back so that he could brush past her.

'How did you find out where I lived?'

'I have my ways. Nice place.' He started heading towards the kitchen and she quickly forestalled him. The fridge was a riot of childish drawings and bits of paper announcing various school happenings. A danger zone, in other words.

'If you want to go into the sitting room, Riccardo, but I can't be long. I'm…I'm on my way out.'

'Clutching a can of furniture polish?'

Charlotte had forgotten about that. 'After I do a bit of dusting, naturally. And change. I do all my housework on a Saturday.'

'I'm surprised your fiancé doesn't help out there. Seems the kind of guy to enjoy a spot of dusting. Where is he anyway?'

'What do you want, Riccardo? Why have you come here?'

'Because you've been on my mind.' Their eyes met, and Charlotte felt a sickening lurch somewhere in her stomach. God, his voice could still do things to her! And looking at him now… He was casually dressed. On most other men, the dark grey trousers and grey jumper would frankly have looked insipid. Riccardo looked devastating. He had a body that was fashioned for those immaculately tailored Italian clothes he wore. Tall, broad shouldered, lean hipped. Charlotte swallowed and told herself to focus.

'Oh yes?'

'Oh yes,' he mimicked her gravely as he sat on one of the sofas and crossed his legs.

Around him the little room, which she had taken so much time and effort to decorate with honey, cream and oatmeal colours, looked average and uninspired. She didn't sit down, preferring to remain hovering by the doorway significantly, even though she felt a mess in her dungarees and thick, padded socks. She had to do something with the hair, though. She needed the comfort of feeling it around her face, providing cover, so she yanked off the Alice band and continued to look at him blandly.

'That was a pretty annoying stunt you pulled the other night,' Riccardo said. 'Letting Lucinda believe that there was more to our liaison than there was.'

'I don't happen to think it's fair the way you treat women. I could tell that she wants more from you than a hop in the sack, and if you can't provide that "more" then you should be upfront.'

'And, just in case I wasn't, you were prepared to jump in and be upfront on my behalf. Or at least land me in as much bother as you could. Payback for bumping into you accidentally after eight years.'

'Okay. If you've come here looking for an apology, then I apologise. Satisfied?'

'No.' Riccardo stretched out his long legs and settled back into the sofa. 'I told you. You've been on my mind.'

Charlotte went across to the chair facing him and flopped bonelessly into it. Standing by the door, trying to be a woman in control, was difficult when your legs felt like jelly. 'I'm not interested, Riccardo.'

'Aren't you? Is that why you're shaking like a leaf? Because you're so *indifferent* to me?' Riccardo watched her nervously sweep her fingers through her hair. He could almost hear the cranking of the gears in her head as she tried to formulate a verbal deterrent. Really and truly, he hadn't known what he was going to say to her once he arrived on her doorstep. Yes, he'd been annoyed at her interference with Lucinda, but that had not been anything he hadn't been able to deal with.

More complex was his reaction to Charlotte. Ever since he had bumped into her, he had been behaving out of character, and for the life of him he couldn't understand why. He just knew that he had resurrected an old relationship with Lucinda to prove to himself that the blonde who had surfaced after eight years meant nothing to him. It hadn't worked, and he couldn't figure out how a man like him, a man who could have any woman he wanted, would find himself going crazy with thoughts of a woman who wanted nothing to do with him.

Bumping into them, seeing her with her fiancé, had clarified at least one piece of the puzzle.

He wanted her. Whether he liked the fact or not. Hence sitting here now, on her sofa, watching her seethe in impotent frustration at his presence in her house.

'Why don't you just tell me what you want, Riccardo? I've apologised over the Lucinda thing, and I meant it. What you do is no business of mine.' But watching him squirm had been worth its weight in gold!

'And what *you* do shouldn't be any business of *mine*, but I find that it is.'

Charlotte felt faint. Out of the corner of her eye she could see the hands of her watch ticking. Time was creeping by and Riccardo was showing no signs of leaving.

In one split instant, she realised that she had made a

fatal error. She had hoped to quench Riccardo's curiosity by producing a fiancé and she had also, she'd thought, killed two birds with one stone because she'd figured that a fiancé would show him just how much her life had moved on.

She should have known that his curiosity over Ben would not have politely stopped the minute she'd hopped in her little car and driven away. Riccardo was not a polite person. If he hadn't bumped into her at that club, then sooner or later he would have tracked her down, because he would have wanted to meet the man he thought she was intimately involved with.

He was staring at her, waiting for her to respond, and knowing that with each passing second of silence her discomfort was increasing.

Casually he let his eyes drift through the room. Pale colours. Not what he would have expected from a woman with a deeply passionate nature, but then maybe she was trying to stifle that passion. A small flat-screen television was perched on top of an antique pine bookcase. And in front of that row of books…

Riccardo stood up and strolled towards the bookcase, then he squatted down and looked at the framed pictures. They were all of the same person. He picked one up and stood up.

'Who is she? That niece of yours in Australia?'

Charlotte literally couldn't answer because her vocal cords seemed to have seized up. Nor could she get to her feet and do something useful like snatch the photo from him. Not when her legs had turned to lead.

Nor did she have to, because as his question hung in

the silence the sound of the doorbell was already answering his question.

'Are you going to get that?' He replaced the photo on the shelf, but remained standing where he was. 'Might be someone important.'

Charlotte stood up shakily and looked at him.

'Yes. Yes, I'm sure it will be…'

CHAPTER FIVE

GINA had been to the corner shop with Amy and her mum and had returned the proud owner of a very large bag of teeth-destroying sweets. Despite a daily diet of healthy foods, and stern chats about the horrors of eating sweets, she still saved her pocket money for her weekly sugar fix. For once, Charlotte didn't frown, shake her head and tell her that there was no way she would be allowed to eat the lot in one go. In fact, she opened the door and stood there, looking at her beautiful daughter who bore such a stunning resemblance to the man sitting in her lounge.

'Are you feeling sick, Mum?' Gina frowned anxiously. 'You could have one of my sweets, if you like,' she said kindly. 'But not any of the orange ones.'

'Come in, baby.'

Gina looked at her mother in alarm. This was not the normal Saturday sweet-buying routine. She popped a Fruit Pastille nervously into her mouth and was even more alarmed when nothing was said. 'I promise I'll tidy my room *right now*,' she declared.

'There's someone I think you need to meet, Gina.'

'Is it Mr Forbes?' Her eyes began to well up. 'Because it wasn't my fault that I forgot to do my homework!'

'You forgot to do your homework?' Charlotte was momentarily distracted, then she remembered Riccardo in the lounge and gave Gina a reassuring smile. 'No, it's not Mr Forbes.' Very gently she helped her daughter out of her puffy black coat, then the black boots, until she was left just in her pair of jeans and long-sleeved black jumper. Charlotte had given up trying to coax her daughter into pink a long time ago.

'Okay?' Charlotte asked, and Gina nodded and slipped another sweet into her mouth which, pleasantly surprised, she got away with.

Charlotte was holding Gina's hand as they walked into the lounge to find Riccardo standing by the window, arms folded. They both stopped by the door and, on a roll, Gina dipped her hand into the bag of sweets, only for Charlotte to relieve her of it and place it on a side table.

'Riccardo, I'd like you to meet Gina.'

Gina stood stock still by her mother's side and stared unblinkingly at the man looking at her.

'That's a pretty name,' Riccardo said, for want of anything better. He had next to no experience of children. As an only child, there had been no nephews or nieces. 'How old you are?' he asked, discomfited by the silence that greeted his trite remark.

'Gina's eight,' Charlotte said quickly, waiting to see if the penny would drop. But of course it didn't. There was no reason for him to think that Gina was *her* daughter, and in the absence of that crucial piece of information she would just be a random kid to him.

She could feel tension clawing its way in her stomach, and she licked her lips and tightened her grip on Gina's hand. Riccardo was beginning to look faintly bored. Didn't he wonder at all what an eight-year-old child was doing in her house?

'I'm in Year Four at St Bart's Primary school,' Gina piped up. 'I'm top of my class in maths *and* english,' she said proudly. 'Last week I got a *star* award!' She looked at Charlotte. 'Didn't I, Mum?'

Charlotte watched as Riccardo's brain shifted into gear, heading towards the inexorable conclusion. He went very, very still and his eyes sharpened on Gina's face, taking in the dark, tumbling curls, the big brown eyes, the slightly olive skin—putting two and two together.

Having broken the ice, Gina, self-assured like her father, began to chat about her star award, offering to fetch it for a viewing, while Riccardo looked at her in frozen silence.

'Eight years old,' he said finally, in an oddly unsteady voice. 'And when exactly is your birthday, Gina?'

'Gina, you need to go and clean that room of yours now… And as a special treat…' Charlotte snatched the bag of sweets from the table and thrust it into her daughter's astounded hand with a strained smile. 'But only this once! Because I need to have a private little chat with Riccardo. So, after you clean your room, you can… you can…' She could feel Riccardo's eyes boring into her, and she didn't need to read the expression in them because her imagination was well equipped to provide it for her. 'You can play on your games console!' Whilst not quite as bad as the sweets issue, Gina's computer games were a limited treat. She grinned happily and didn't wait for her mother to change her mind which, she had discovered, adults had a way of doing. She dashed up the stairs, and Charlotte closed the door gently behind her. She had to lean against the closed door to support herself.

'Oh, dear God, tell me that you weren't… Dios! Tell me that you weren't pregnant…' Riccardo said in a flat, stunned voice. For the first time in his life he felt as though life had turned around and kicked him in the stomach, and then, having done so, had returned to repeat the exercise. He sat down heavily on the sofa and rested his elbows on his knees. The thoughts in his head were moving so quickly that he felt physically sick. He dropped his head in his hands and stared down at the floor.

'Look,' Charlotte said awkwardly. 'I didn't mean for you to find out this way.' She took a couple of tentative steps towards the chair, and Riccardo turned his head to look at her with savage contempt.

'What you're saying is that you didn't mean for me to find out at *all*!' That small dark-haired child whom he had viewed with just mild curiosity was his own *flesh and blood*! Riccardo felt a surge of rage wash through him with the force of a tidal wave, and he had to breathe deeply or else succumb to a violence he had never felt before. Which wouldn't do. Already his mind was working quickly, trying to figure out how best to handle the unbelievable.

Charlotte didn't say anything. He was beginning to scare her, not because she felt he might become physically threatening, but because there was a coldness in his eyes that was even more menacing. 'You don't understand!' she said defensively.

'Then why don't you enlighten me?'

Charlotte could see that the last thing he wanted was enlightenment. He was not going to be prepared to listen to what she had to say, but there was no way that she was going to remain silent.

Riccardo watched as she walked tentatively towards the chair. She looked as though one false move on his part and she would run a mile, and she would be right, he thought, because right now his precious self-control was wearing very thin at the edges. His head was cluttered with images of the child who had told him about her star award, to whom he had shown only passing, polite interest.

'When I left Italy I had no idea that I was pregnant,' Charlotte said tightly. 'We were so careful. Just a couple of times. Well, that was all it took. '

'And so, when you discovered that you were, you just decided that you would eliminate me from the picture,' Ricardo said, his voice cold and steady.

'You made it perfectly clear that I had been a passing fling. You didn't need your life cluttered up with a clingy girlfriend. The last thing you would want would be your life cluttered up with a responsibility that would last a lifetime.'

'My own child.' Riccardo tried to get his head around that and found that he couldn't. 'How *dare* you sit there and calmly tell me what I would or would not have wanted when it came to my own flesh and blood!'

'And how dare you sit there and imply that what I did was a deliberate act of cruelty!' Charlotte returned hotly.

She glanced at the closed door and lowered her voice, because children had a knack of appearing just when you didn't want them to. 'I was in pieces when I left Italy. How do you imagine *I* felt when I found out that I was pregnant, alone here, with no means of income and a university career that was over before it had had a chance to begin? Don't you think that I wished I could turn to you for support?' Charlotte took a bitter trip down memory lane. 'Yes, I admit it briefly crossed my mind to get in touch with you, although that would have been difficult enough. Every time the thought crossed my mind, I imagined what your reaction would be. To not want someone to be part of your life and then find out that you're lumbered with their offspring…'

'That's no excuse! What kind of monster do you think I am, that I would deny my own child?'

'Actually there are quite a few men who turn tail and run the minute they know their girlfriend's pregnant. Believe me, it's not exactly a unique reaction!'

'I am not "quite a few men"!'

Charlotte took a deep breath and looked at him. 'I was scared, Riccardo. I had walked out of a lion's den. I wasn't about to head straight back into it. You didn't want me…' God, it still hurt even now to say that. 'You didn't want me, and the way I saw it was that, even if I went straight back to Italy and broke the happy news to you, you would either send me on my way again or else take my baby away from me!'

'*Our* baby!'

'There's no point getting into a great big argument about it now, Riccardo. What's done is done.'

'It never occurred to tell me at *any point* along the way that I was a father?'

'I built my life without you. It's not like I chose the easy option.'

Riccardo stood up abruptly, so abruptly that it took a few seconds for Charlotte to register that he was going. But going where?

'You're not taking my daughter away from me!' She sprang to her feet, ready to do anything it took to avert that eventuality. 'Don't imagine that you can use your money and influence to have Gina!'

'I cannot stay under this roof a minute longer,' Riccardo said savagely. 'I need to go away and think.'

'Think about what?' She reached for his arm, and he shrugged her away.

'I'll be back, and when I return, believe me, I will come with a solution!'

'A solution?' What kind of solution? Did he imagine that this was an intriguing little conundrum that could be sorted out, the way he sorted out his problems at work?

But she was relieved that he wasn't storming up the stairs, two at a time, so that he could shake Gina's world to its foundations. Although, she knew that the time had come to tell her daughter about her dad. Of course she had asked questions in the past, but really not that many. They had been content to live in their happy little bubble, and Charlotte had shoved the future and all its attendant problems, when Gina got older and grew more curious, to the back of her mind.

But she would wait a while, and over the next four days the waiting nearly killed her. She lived on her nerves, expecting the doorbell to go at any moment, with Riccardo and his lawyer standing on her doorstep demanding custody, even though she knew, thinking rationally, that there was no way he could pull that off. But, then again, Riccardo could pull off anything or at least that was the impression he gave.

In the end, she telephoned Aubrey and bared her soul. She wanted to hear him soothe all those irrational fears away, which he did, but it wasn't enough. She had to find out what Riccardo was up to; she had to steal his march.

'Aubrey, I just have to know where he is. I have to get in touch with him.'

'Leave it with me.'

And less than two hours later she knew. All those years, and she could have bumped into him at any time. She had lived her life in blissful ignorance of the danger lurking virtually on her doorstep. Because his offices were in London, not a million miles away from where she worked, and shockingly close to a couple of penthouse suites she had sold to overseas investors. They probably would have bumped into each other at that jazz club much earlier if she had had any kind of active social life. She knew the area well, as he no doubt did too, and they both loved jazz.

Of course, she knew that he would probably not have spent all of his time in London, but still.

It took all her courage to take the bull by its horns and confront Riccardo on his own turf. It had been bad enough dealing with him in the safe confines of her own house, but, as she dressed carefully for the meeting she had never really anticipated, she could feel her stomach work itself into a series of knots.

Her normal morning routine had a nightmarish feel to it, and she had even sent Gina off to school with a chocolate bar nestled next to her sandwich and yoghurt. Then she had looked at herself in the mirror, a long, hard look. Not that it would make a scrap of difference, she wanted to present herself as a model human being. Fat chance of him falling in line with *that* plan, she thought, heading out and hailing the first taxi she could find so that she didn't have to battle with the underground.

She didn't know whether he would be in or not, and, as the taxi dropped her off in front of one of those paeans to modern architecture that left her cold, she half hoped that he would be out—somewhere safely abroad, tucked away on a continent far from her and Gina.

However, if he did happen to be around, then she was pretty certain that she would be ushered up to his office the minute she gave her name. A bit like a rabbit being shown straight to the lion's den.

It was an analogy she wished she hadn't thought of, as the girl at Reception put through a call and was told that Mr di Napoli was indeed in and, yes, having been given Charlotte's name, he would see her.

Better than that, his secretary would fetch her from Reception! The girl at the desk looked at Charlotte with new-found respect. Maybe the neatly turned out blonde with the frankly unadventurous outfit had a bit more going for her than she'd originally thought.

Charlotte's unadventurous outfit had been planned for a purpose. The purpose was to show Riccardo that when it came to Gina she meant business, that she was not going to be steamrollered by him, but neither was her intention to wage war or go on the immediate attack. Hence she had decided on a suit in a sensible colour. Grey. But it was a trouser suit, and she was wearing a cheerful burgundy jumper with the trousers.

Now if she could only get her mind to be as relaxed and confident as her outfit, she thought as the elevator purred its way up to the top floor, she might be getting somewhere.

But her mind refused to be reined in. Riccardo *affected* her. She wished it was simply a case of hate, which was what she had been at pains to imply, combined with a healthy dose of apprehension and resentment at the situation in which she now found herself, but there was something else. It was like a dangerous snake rustling in the undergrowth, and Charlotte knew that there was still an attraction there for her. Worse, she suspected that it had always been there, just lying in wait, and now that he had shown up on the scene it had surfaced and was gathering force.

Poor Ben. She had seen him the evening before and had apologetically told him that he should think of finding someone else.

'I don't deserve you, Ben,' Charlotte had said truthfully, reaching across the table and linking her fingers through his. 'You're a nice guy, and you need a woman who doesn't come with an armful of complications.'

'You mean a woman who doesn't come with a rival.'

'No!' She'd made a dismissive, snorting noise. 'Riccardo? A rival? Not in a million years! But I'm in a messy situation just at the moment, and it's not fair that you get caught up in the undertow.'

'Maybe it's a good thing that he knows about Gina.'

'You wouldn't say that if you knew the man.' She had been pleased and relieved that Ben had taken it so well. In fact, they had parted on the best possible terms, agreeing to remain friends. Later she wondered whether he could ever have been right for her, or she right for him, if breaking up had been such a painless affair.

The elevator shuddered to a stop. She was aware that Riccardo's secretary had been making polite conversation with her, and she wondered whether she could get away with murmuring something vague because the last thing she needed was a chat with someone she didn't know. Not when she was fighting to control her desire to run away. She wondered what the pleasant, middle-aged, grey-haired woman would say if she blurted out the truth: that she had come to discuss her boss's parental visiting rights to his eight-year-old daughter. How much greyer could grey hair turn?

Riccardo's office was at the very end of a long corridor, on either side of which thick doors alerted the uninitiated that the people sitting behind them were *very* important. The double-fronted wooden doors at the end of the corridor thereby sent the clear message that the person behind them was *beyond* very important.

And of course, Charlotte thought as his secretary pushed open the door, a beyond-very-important man wouldn't do something as crazily simple as come to the door to greet them. He would be staring out of his virtually floor-to-ceiling glass windows at all those small, lesser folk tramping the city streets below, as Riccardo was now doing.

She heard the door shut gently behind her and took a deep breath as Riccardo slowly turned around. For him, the past few days had seen him suffer the agonies of confusion that everyone endures at various points in their lives, but which for him were novel and unwelcome emotions. He could count on the fingers of one hand the number of hours' sleep he had had, and he was functioning at work on automatic level.

He had given himself nearly a week to absorb the situation, because he really hadn't trusted himself to return to her house and deal with it in a controlled and adult manner. Now he was glad that she had appeared on his doorstep, so to speak, because she was in his territory. He recalled that feeling of trying to walk in quicksand when he had been at her house, as he had watched the foundations of his orderly world disappear out of reach, and his mouth tightened.

'I realise you said that you would be in touch,' Charlotte said without bothering with any phoney pleasantries. 'But I can't just sit around and wait until you decide the time is right to come knocking on my door with your so-called "solution".'

'Sit.' It was a command rather than an invitation, and Charlotte momentarily hesitated, not liking the fact that he was issuing orders. He had never been like this years ago, had he? Then she told herself that it was not in her interests to keep remembering the man who he had once been. It distracted her from the man who he now was, and this was the man she had to keep at a distance, whatever physical connection existed between them in the form of their daughter.

She sat and was relieved when he followed suit, although in his case it was behind his grand desk, which was a feat of modern carpentry, multi-grained wood with lines so smooth that it looked untouched by human hand.

'So?' Riccardo pushed himself away from the desk so that he could cross his legs at an angle, then he looked at her, in no rush to break the silence. Of course, he was mildly interested in what she had to say and would certainly give her her chance to speak, but already he knew his solution. As he had watched her hovering there by the door, it had come to him as an almost inevitable conclusion.

'I don't want to talk about the past. I know how you feel, I know you think that I should somehow have appeared heavily pregnant on your mother's doorstep, even if I was terrified that you would have taken my baby away from me. I guess, in your mind, I should have been prepared to do that as well. I was just a scared, disillusioned kid, but I should have mustered up the courage and taken whatever was doled out to me by you and your mother.'

Riccardo scowled. Put like that, he could feel a reluctant sympathy. In fact, put like that, he didn't much care for the person he had been eight years ago. He was guiltily aware of how terrifying it must have been for her to have shown up unannounced, only to find her arrival greeted with rejection. Of course, that was no excuse to have denied him his rights as a father, but he could reluctantly see her point of view.

'But I didn't, and, yes, don't imagine that I didn't think about letting you know when Gina was born, when she was growing up.'

'But you successfully managed to squash the temptation.'

'Temptation isn't exactly the word I would have used,' Charlotte admitted truthfully. 'It felt more like a duty that I just…well, could put off. I imagined how you would react, and it was easier to walk away from dealing with the situation.'

'Would you *ever* have mustered the courage or would you have been happy to let sleeping dogs lie—maybe tell Gina that her father had died, make up some story when she started asking too many questions?'

Charlotte looked at him with genuine horror. 'What kind of person do you think I am?'

'The kind who takes the easy way out!'

'Not to the point of lying to Gina about you! I always knew that sooner or later she would demand to know who you were, and I was prepared for that!'

Riccardo didn't point out that by that indeterminate point in the future he would have been a complete stranger to his daughter, and the possibility of any bonding would have been close to zero. She was right. It would be easy to become locked in perpetual arguing over who had been right and who had been wrong, but in the end there was fault on both sides.

Although, he told himself piously, *he* had obviously been the loser.

'So you came here to tell me…?' Riccardo dragged the matter out of the boxing ring and back into civilised territory.

Charlotte took a deep breath. She had given the matter a great deal of thought. 'I think I should be the one to tell

Gina about you.' She held up her hand to stave off an interruption that hadn't been voiced. 'And then you can meet her. Of course, you'll want to get to know her...'

Charlotte had visions of Riccardo becoming a semi-permanent figure in her life, a man who didn't want her but was tied to her because of an accident that had happened in the past. Would he resent her more and more as time went on? How would she feel when he got married, had children of his own? 'And I'm not going to stand in your way. We can work out the nuts and bolts of where and when, but basically I'm willing to be generous with access. Also—' she had nearly forgotten this point '—I don't want any money from you. Eight years ago your mother accused me of being a gold-digger, even though I told her that I hadn't known your financial background, and—'

'When?' Riccardo asked sharply.

'When she showed me up to that room.'

'I didn't know.'

Charlotte shrugged. 'It doesn't matter now, but you need to understand that I don't want anything from you. Nothing. Not a penny.'

His mother had done more damage than he had thought. What else had she said? She was frail now after a fall, but would still be too proud to admit to having made errors in the way she had handled the situation way back then. Another unwilling tug of sympathy.

He stood up and strolled across to the window, which had splendid views over London. For a few seconds he idly followed the progress of people scurrying across pavements as he marshalled his thoughts, then he turned around to look at her.

'So I see my daughter, say, once a week? Twice a week? When I happen to be in London? Because I travel a hell of a lot. And how long do I see her for?—maybe an hour or two after school? Because she would have homework to do, I suppose.'

'There *are* weekends,' Charlotte pointed out, not liking the direction of his comments, or his tone of voice. 'You could see her every other weekend…'

'Except when she's going out, I guess.'

'Why are you making this difficult, Riccardo? It works for loads of other people.'

Riccardo shrugged and walked towards her. For a tall, muscular man his movements had always been graceful and economic, but she still felt to cringe back in the chair, especially when he leant over her and placed his hands on either side of her, palms gripping the arms of her chair.

Up close like this he literally did take her breath away. It was as if she had to create a force field to ward off his dynamism, and she could just about have succeeded, but the minute he closed the physical gap between them she had no protection against the stark power of his presence.

'But not for me. It doesn't work for me, Charlie.'

Charlotte didn't have the strength to remind him that she no longer used that abbreviated nickname. She felt trapped by those amazing eyes with their idiotically long lashes. She used to tease him about that!

'No?' she managed to croak.

'No. I don't intend to be one of those part-time dads, trying to forge a bond for four hours a week. Nor do I intend to watch another man raise my own flesh and blood.'

It took a few seconds for Charlotte to realise that he was talking about Ben. She opened her mouth to protest, but he wasn't about to let her interrupt. She had had her say. Now it was time for his.

'Gina is my daughter, and she will take my name and have all the privileges that are her due!'

'What are you saying?' Charlotte whispered.

'We will be married. Of course. That way I will see my child and be responsible for her on a full-time basis.' He thrust himself away from her and Charlotte remained in a little pool of stupefied silence.

Eventually she said, 'You're kidding, aren't you?'

'Why would you think that?' He perched on his desk and stared down at her.

'Because it's a ridiculous suggestion?'

'To you, maybe. To me, it makes perfect sense. I can give Gina everything she could possibly need or want, and in addition I would have her there, would be able to fulfil my fatherly duties full time, have a say in the decisions that will affect her as the years go by. We get married, and you won't have to work. You can be a full-time mother. There are no drawbacks to this plan. So you can wipe that expression off your face.'

'And my role would be…?'

'You're her mother, of course. Your role in her life would remain unchanged.'

'But aside from that every other aspect of my life would be turned on its head, but that would be okay just so long as you get your own way.'

'There's no point arguing about it, Charlie. We will be married.'

'When did you become like this, Riccardo?'

'Like what?'

'Arrogant. Intransigent. Thinking that you can have whatever you want with the click of a finger.'

Riccardo flushed darkly and glared at her. 'Because I'm not soft? Because I don't subscribe to the theory that men should not be ashamed to cry? That doesn't make me arrogant.' But he *was* arrogant, and the admission made him wince inwardly. 'My solution would be for the best.'

'You solution is insane!' She stood up and controlled the shaking of her hands by dusting off some non-existent specks of fluff from her trousers. 'I know you feel that I've deprived you of time you should have spent with Gina, but I won't allow you to steal my life because you want to create a false family unit.'

'Steal your life?'

'That's right.' She looked at him squarely in the face without flinching. 'Marriage at all costs for the sake of a child might be the Italian way, Riccardo. But it's not mine.'

CHAPTER SIX

AND they hadn't even got around to his fulminating diatribe about the fiancé!

Riccardo glared at the bottle of wine staring reproachfully at him from his gleaming black, granite kitchen counter. One glass for Dutch courage, something he had never needed in his life before, but which he seemed to need now because he was about to see his daughter for the first time.

After her incredulous rejection of his marriage proposal—something he fancied very few women would have turned down without even bothering to give it a second thought—Charlotte had stalked out of his office and he had stayed put, imprisoned by his own pride which had absolutely forbidden him to follow her, beg her to reconsider and listen to the advantages. The obvious advantages.

Four hours later he had phoned and coldly told her that he would respect her ridiculous refusal to listen to common sense, but he'd demanded that she tell Gina about him.

'Of course I will,' Charlotte had said, for all the world

as though anything else would have been incomprehensible. 'And you can come and visit with her tomorrow after school. I don't want to fight you over this, Riccardo.'

'Very generous,' he had muttered with heavy sarcasm, but the arrangement had been made and now here he was, as nervous as a kid waiting to be seen by the headmaster. He swept his trench coat from the counter, drank the contents of his wine glass in one long gulp and headed out of the door.

He had a driver on permanent call, but this time he would be taking a black cab. George was as perfect a driver as he could hope to find, which meant that he never asked questions and could be counted on for his discretion, but a secret child? That might have been taking temptation too far, and Riccardo needed to come to terms with the situation himself before opening the door to the inevitable furore of gossip.

On the way, staring out at the dark, bleak and cluttered city streets, he marshalled his wayward thoughts into coherent points. Point one would be elimination of the fiancé. He wasn't going to share his child with another man and that was just something she would have to accept.

Since when, he wondered, had she become so damned *mouthy*?

He frowned and thought of her glowering in his office, *laughing* at his proposal and then refusing to budge! Indeed, walking out!

Well, the fiancé would be a thing of the past if he had to set up camp in her house and supervise her movements like a babysitter!

The taxi drew up outside the house and nerves ripped through him like a knife. He had bought a stuffed toy. A very large one. What else did one buy for a child with whom you were intimately connected and yet didn't know you from Adam?

He felt utterly foolish and stupidly terrified as he pressed the doorbell and heard it reverberate inside the house.

Charlotte opened the door, and behind her was Gina.

'What on earth is that?' Charlotte smiled reluctantly at the sight of Riccardo clutching an oversized brown-and-white stuffed dog. It was a very floppy stuffed animal and its limbs drooped over his hands as though it had decided to fall into a deep sleep, leaving its owner slightly bewildered as to what he was doing with the thing in the first place.

'It's a dog.'

'Gina, come and meet—'

'I…I brought you this…' Riccardo heard himself stumble over his words and he looked to Charlotte for help.

'It's gorgeous, isn't it, Gina? Come in. Look at this dog! It's the biggest stuffed animal I've ever seen! It's almost as big as your room, honey. Where are you going to put it? You should thank your…your…'

'Dad,' Gina said, one eye on the dog, one eye on Riccardo. She smiled shyly and took the dog, and all at once Riccardo felt foolishly, ridiculously happy. Nothing like the sort of happy he felt when he closed a deal or staged a takeover. This was a feeling that penetrated through to parts of him he hadn't known were there.

'Why don't you go upstairs and show…show your dad where you're going to put that wonderful dog.'

It was as easy as that. The door closed behind him, he removed his coat and followed his daughter up to her room. Both threw Charlotte a look of hesitancy, but Charlotte ignored that. She had told Gina about her father, had glossed over the whys and wherefores, and had left so many threads dangling that it was a wonder she hadn't become entangled in her own story. But Gina had not asked any awkward questions. Her childish eyes had lit up, and for the first time Charlotte had realised how much of a disservice she had done her daughter, although every decision made had been made in good faith.

She closed her eyes and sagged against the banister, then after a few minutes up she went, hearing their voices before she appeared in the doorway.

Gina was showing him her handheld games console, which had been her last birthday present, and explaining how it worked while Riccardo listened in what appeared to be fascinated silence.

For a few seconds Charlotte watched the scenario, then she cleared her throat and they both looked round at her.

'I thought it might be nice if we went out for a meal,' she said.

'Fish and chips?' Gina asked hopefully. 'Do you like fish and chips, Dad?'

'I…I love it.'

'Nice try,' Charlotte said dryly. She looked at Riccardo in a moment of unthinking shared honesty at the wiles of an eight-year-old. 'We try and limit the greasy food, so we'll take you to the Italian on the corner. They do a very nice, and very healthy, *pomodoro* pasta.'

'Mum hates junk food. Do you hate junk food?'

'Junk food?' Riccardo asked.

'That's not something your dad's probably ever had in his life before.'

'You've *never* had junk food? *Ever?*' On which subject Gina maintained a steady and incredulous conversation as they gathered up their coats and headed out of the house, Riccardo on one side, Charlotte on the other and Gina between them.

'What do you eat, then?' she demanded as they perused the menu and she perused them.

'Oh, all sorts of things.' Riccardo smiled, liking her directness but alarmed by it as well. 'Mostly I eat out.'

'Isn't that very expensive?'

'Gina, please!'

'Mum says you're not married. Do you have a girlfriend?'

'Well, no.'

Gina smiled triumphantly at both of them, but before she could really and truly put her eight-year-old feet firmly in it Charlotte said hurriedly, 'And let's just leave it there.'

She looked at Riccardo and could see him processing his daughter's stray remark, putting it somewhere safe for future reference.

Later, with an overtired and overexcited Gina finally in bed, Charlotte made her way downstairs to find Riccardo in the kitchen, scrutinising all the childish bits of schoolwork that had been stuck to the noticeboard on the wall behind the kitchen table.

'I thought that went okay,' she said cautiously.

'I think we need to talk.'

'What about?' Charlotte had seen hundreds of sides of Riccardo in the past, all the bits and pieces that went to make up this complex man, but she now realised that she had only ever seen a fraction of what he was all about—because tonight had been a revelation. She had watched him listen with humour and consideration, and ask questions to which he patently knew the answers. It had been a bizarre situation, a brush with true domesticity that she had never had. There had been times during the course of the evening when she had had to remind herself that they weren't a happy little family unit straight out of *The Waltons*, but two people united in a false situation for the sake of their child.

'Where to begin?'

'Not with accusations.'

'Then let's start with this fiancé of yours, shall we?'

'Okay, but—'

'No, no *buts*, Charlie.' Riccardo thought of the way his daughter laughed, the way she grinned, the way she pulled herself up straight when she thought she was on the verge of making an important point to adults. When he thought of another man sharing those moments, he felt physically ill.

'You kept my daughter from me for eight years. You tell me you won't marry me, allow me to legitimise my own daughter, and I can't force you to walk up an aisle with me.'

She thought he looked as though he'd like to have given it a good try, however.

'I explained that.'

'Keep quiet!' He banged his fist on the kitchen table and Charlotte jumped. 'I… Tonight has been one of the hardest nights of my entire life. I've had to watch my daughter and wonder at all the missed years.' He looked at her and raked his fingers through his hair. 'I won't have another man bring my child up.'

'There's no question of that,' Charlotte said quickly.

'You get rid of him, do you understand me?'

I already have. 'Or else what?' She folded her arms and stuck her chin up.

'Or else,' Riccardo growled, 'I'll move into this house, lock stock and barrel, and set up camp! Would you like that? My computer taking over the kitchen table? My shoes at the bottom of the stairs? I know Gina wouldn't mind. Did you see her eyes light up when I told her that her daddy didn't have a girlfriend? How do you think she'd react if I asked her whether she wanted me and her mother to live together?' Okay, he knew it was below the belt, but that stubbornness was driving him crazy and even worse was the suspicion that the touchy-feely boyfriend was to blame. Eight years ago one touch and she'd been his. Now he was the dinosaur, deposed by someone who could cook a mean quiche.

'That's not fair!' Charlotte said hotly.

'Then lose the boyfriend.' Riccardo stood up, but there was precious little room in the kitchen. He felt hemmed in and suddenly in need of a drink. He had dutifully stuck to water during the meal. Now he opened her fridge and extracted a half-full bottle of supermarket white wine.

'Make yourself at home,' Charlotte said sarcastically.

'Oh, believe me, I intend to. Where do you keep your glasses?'

'Sit down. I'll get them.' She reached up and her jumper rose, exposing a slither of skin. Riccardo found himself savouring the tantalising glimpse. 'You think it's all right for me to disrupt my life, chuck a guy I happen to like a great deal?'

'*Like?* That says it all, Charlie.'

'Stop calling me that!'

'Why? Because it reminds you too much of when we were young and couldn't get enough of one another?'

Suddenly it was as if the oxygen had been sucked out of the tiny kitchen. A sense of erotic, forbidden intimacy shoved its way through the tense atmosphere, and her hand was shaking as she put his glass of wine in front of him and took a hearty swig of hers.

'You're going to *marry* a guy because you *like* him?' Riccardo gave a snort of derisive laughter that made her hackles rise.

'Affection happens to be a very important part of a relationship!'

'So is passion, and I didn't witness much of that when I saw the two of you together!'

'Well, we weren't all over each other like a *rash*, if that's what you mean! And, on the subject of other halves, now that you're laying down laws, what about *your* other half? The Amazonian bimbo with the tight outfit—is she really out of the picture or was that just a fairy story for Gina's benefit?'

'What makes you think that she's a bimbo?' Riccardo asked with interest.

'Oh, sorry. Was I mistaken? Is she a nuclear physicist?'

'No, not quite,' he admitted. 'Actually, I would be surprised if she could even spell it.'

Charlotte looked at him over the rim of her wine glass and grinned reluctantly. 'Well?'

'No fairy story. I've already got rid of her.'

'You're kidding.'

'No, I'm not. And it was a hell of a lot harder than it should have been, considering you laid it on thick about love and marriage and a non-existent future.'

'Sorry. I couldn't resist.' Charlotte knew that this pause in hostilities was a dangerous no-man's-land. It was too easy to see the man she had fallen head over heels in love with and she didn't want to go there again. Any arrangements they now had would be strictly along business lines. 'You shouldn't have descended on us.'

'Oh, but I had to. I had to size up the competition.'

'There's no competition.'

Riccardo felt a flare of rage. He couldn't understand what the hell she saw in the man, and he noticed that she had yet to confirm that she would be ditching him. 'We don't have to get married. Yet. But I want us to live together. That way we can give Gina the family unit she's missed for the past eight years.'

'No!'

'Why not? Does the man live with you?'

'No, of course not!'

'Then what's the problem?'

'Don't you get it, Riccardo?' She finished the glass of wine. Now she fancied another. 'Yes, it's important for Gina to have both of us, and now that she's met you

I recognise that you're here to stay when it comes to her. But you just have to look at it from the point of view of a divorced person involved in an amicable joint-custody type situation.' Charlotte took a deep breath and looked him directly in the eyes, which made her feel a bit giddy.

'I don't want to marry you or live with you because… because…we just don't have that kind of relationship. Marriage and co-habitation should be about commitment and sharing, and *wanting* to be together. It shouldn't be a duty undertaken because of force of circumstance, if you know what I mean.' She pushed her hand through her hair and leaned on the table. 'When I say "I do" to a marriage or even to a guy moving in with me, I want to feel excited about it.'

Riccardo flushed darkly. 'Most marriages end in divorce. People start out with stars in their eyes, and then reality sets in and they find they can't deal with it. What's wrong with a business arrangement? It makes sense.'

'Not to me. And we're just going round in circles here, Riccardo.' She gave in to temptation and poured herself another glass of wine. 'I don't want to marry you and I don't want to live with you.'

'There was a time when you would have jumped at the prospect.'

'That was a long time ago.' She rested the glass on the table and ran her finger lightly around the rim. 'I was a different person then and so were you. We've both changed.'

'You mean you became a responsible adult who decided that a passion-free relationship with a man who doesn't challenge you is the safe, logical way to go.'

'Ben is *very* challenging!'

'Don't get me wrong, Charlie. I'm not saying that he isn't a thoroughly *nice* guy…'

Charlotte gritted her teeth. He managed in those few words to paint a picture of someone mind-numbingly dull, and she momentarily regretted her elaborate and fictitious description of a man who was sensitive and in touch with his feminine side.

'I *like* nice, Riccardo.'

'Because it's safe?'

'Yes, it's safe, and what's wrong with that?'

'Nothing. But right now…' Riccardo leaned towards her, every muscle in his body taut with menacing intent. 'Life's a little *unconventional*, wouldn't you agree? And unconventional situations call for unconventional solutions. Besides…' Riccardo relaxed back into the chair and twirled his wine glass lazily in his hand. 'What we had was pretty strong, if I recall; who knows if it's all still there, lying just beneath the surface? One touch and *pow*!' He made a little explosive gesture with his hand and then deliberately looked at her very slowly, a leisurely, sexual exploration that made her skin burn.

'Don't be ridiculous,' Charlotte said, clearing her throat. This was just another ploy to try and get what he wanted, whatever the cost! She pushed herself up and looked at her watch. 'When would you like to next visit Gina?'

'You still haven't told me what you intend to do about the boyfriend.'

'I'll obviously think about what you've asked, Riccardo, but I won't be turning my life upside down just to suit you. You might sneer at Ben because he's not like you, but you might also want to stop and think that he's exactly what I need. And want!' she added belatedly. She folded her arms and backed towards the kitchen door, bumping into the doorframe as Riccardo took a step towards her. She dearly hoped that the madness swirling around inside her wasn't reflected on her face.

'Hmm. Interesting,' Riccardo drawled. One step closer. 'Because you don't look all that convinced of what you're saying.'

'I mean…' now he was standing right in front of her, trapping her with her back pressed hard against the wall '…your colour's all up.'

'What can you expect?' Charlotte said wildly. 'I mean, you sit there asking all sorts of impossible things!'

'Making all sorts of impossible allusions,' Riccardo agreed on a husky note. 'Daring to suggest that we can still *do* things to each other…' He reached out and feathered a finger along her cheek. To Charlotte, it was like being brushed by a flame. She twisted her head away but her heart was pounding and her body… Her body was on fire, alive with a whirlwind of responses that she hadn't felt for anyone since *him*!

She breathed in deeply, nostrils flaring, made herself remember the crucial footnote to his behaviour which was that he was using her to get what he desperately wanted. He wasn't attracted to *her*!

'I'll call you, Riccardo.'

'Not good enough, I'm afraid. You're trembling. Why? Does the boyfriend make you tremble like this? Do you know that I can breathe you in? I remember the smell—of Italy and summer and your skin.'

'Don't!' It had meant to sound like a forceful command.

Instead it sounded like a plea. She placed one hand squarely on his chest, which was a bit of a tactical error, because instantly she was flooded with memories of how he looked bare-backed, his muscles tightly packed.

'Why not? Scared?'

'You can't just come in here and do whatever you want.'

'No, but I am happy to do whatever *you* want.' And she wanted him. Riccardo could feel it. He was also achingly aware of how much he wanted *her*. Quite honestly, he had felt the pull the minute he had clapped eyes on her. He wondered now if he had ever really stopped wanting her. Yes he had turned away, because at the time he'd been convinced that a serious relationship was not what he wanted, least of all with a kid who had lied to him about his age, but he had never sought to replace her, had he? He should have forgotten about her, moved on to have a stable relationship with someone; Lord knew it was what his mother had spent years clamouring for. But he hadn't. Instead, he had littered his life with a series of pointless bimbos. Now, here, breathing this woman in, he felt at ease with himself.

He leaned down, brushed her lips with his, and she tried to wriggle free but not with any conviction.

This was madness! She wanted to pull him to her and sink herself into his kiss. Instead, she pushed him away and found that she was panting as he straightened up and looked down at her.

'Tomorrow,' Riccardo said.

'Tomorrow?'

'I'll be in touch.'

Well, he thought as he stepped out into the bleak

blackness to hail a cab, she hadn't left him very much choice, had she?

Yes, she had given him a long speech about Mr Right, but he knew this much: Mr Right was not Mr Fiancé. She might think that safety and predictability were qualities she was after, but she was wrong. He had felt it just then in her trembling struggle to tear herself away from him.

And she hadn't told him what he had wanted to hear, that her relationship with Ben would be off. She had skilfully danced around the subject, and he had left none the wiser as to what her intentions were. But when he thought back to their conversation, he was sickly aware that running towards him, arms outstretched, for the sake of their daughter was just not enough for her.

Riccardo, accustomed as he was to life conforming to exactly what he wanted, was afflicted by an unexpected attack of mortal fear.

So what if she'd felt a little edge of nostalgic attraction to him? What did it mean? Nothing. Because she had emerged from her disastrous, disillusioning relationship with him into something she had convinced herself she wanted to be, and the fact that *he* was convinced otherwise meant nothing.

He would end up being a part-time father, taking Gina out to fast-food restaurants and trying to bond with her in two-hour sessions once a week. And eventually Ben—stolid, reliable, 'let me cook for you honey' Ben—would get his foot in through the front door until he became the full-time dad doing homework with Gina, watching her grow up, sorting out her problems.

It wouldn't happen at once. She would do her utmost

to accommodate him, because he knew that she felt guilty, but gradually the guilt would begin to fade and then the relationship that she might have put on hold would resurface. Riccardo knew human nature, knew that good intentions had a very short life span and guilt an even shorter one.

So then he came right back to his original question—what choice had she left him?

The brilliant thing about money was the way it could buy things you couldn't see or touch. Speed, for instance. A couple of calls and he had made all the necessary arrangements to have the paraphernalia of the home office ready to be installed the following afternoon.

He could have just made do with his laptop computer, but that would have felt like a temporary option, so he had gone the whole hog, including an extra telephone line and broadband internet access.

He telephoned her office promptly the following afternoon and told her to meet him at her house in an hour.

On the other end of the line, Charlotte overcame the jolt to her nervous system on hearing his voice and prepared to bristle, but he had already hung up, leaving her no option but to rearrange the meeting she had scheduled with two mortgage specialists and leave the office in the capable but slightly dippy hands of her second in command.

She was unprepared for what met her eyes: vans. Men in overalls. Items of equipment. And, of course, Riccardo in the midst of it all.

Charlotte dropped her briefcase and stared, open

mouthed, barely aware of Riccardo walking in her direction.

'I know,' he said, sticking his hands into his trouser pockets. 'Utter chaos. But once everyone's inside we can leave them to get on with things, and by the time we get back, hey presto, you'll never know they've been!' Riccardo looked at her warily. Yes, of course he had everything under control, but the woman, as he was finding out, was feisty, unpredictable and not of a disposition to take things lying down.

'Riccardo, *what's going on*?'

'But we can't get in without a key.'

Charlotte reached into her bag without thinking. Anything to sort out the Piccadilly Circus situation on her doorstep.

From her own front door, she watched in dazed silence as Riccardo took charge. Events seemed to be moving at the speed of sound, men expertly checking things, stooping and peering under bits of furniture, then after what seemed like a lifetime Riccardo joined her by the front door wearing a sympathetic expression, which should have warned her of underhand dealings, but she was still too flummoxed to pay attention to that.

'Now, here's my idea,' Riccardo said. 'We go and get Gina from school and go somewhere…fun. And warm.' He was liking what he saw. Charlotte in her work clothes, and not spitting fire at him, was incredibly appealing. She looked so damn *young* to be carrying a briefcase and wearing a stern grey suit. Her eyes looked enormous.

'Fun? Warm? What are you talking about? And

what's going on in my house? Who were all those men?' He was already ushering her into the back seat of a black cab, which seemed to have appeared from nowhere, and asking her for the name of Gina's school. It was literally a short walking distance from the house, something for which Riccardo was deeply thankful, as he could sense Charlotte's shock beginning to wear off.

It was peculiar, but he had always been intolerant of women who were demanding or argumentative. As far as he was concerned, his working life was high octane and stressful enough without his brief windows of relaxation being spent listening to a nagging harpy. The role of a woman was to soothe. In Charlotte's case, however, he found himself oddly invigorated by her outspoken and frankly unwelcome disregard for his personal boundaries. Maddened, but invigorated. Right now he could see her edging towards a major outburst, but fortunately the black cab was pulling up outside the primary school.

Charlotte looked at him in exasperation, fully aware that the taxi driver was ready and willing to sit in on a long-winded rant with his meter running.

'I'll be ten minutes,' she warned him. 'And when I get back you'd better have a few answers for me!'

'Yes, ma'am!'

Charlotte made an inarticulate sound of pure annoyance as she saw Riccardo and the cab driver exchange one of those infuriating eyes-to-the-heavens 'who knows women?' looks.

Yes, her life had been a bit boring, a bit lacking in something vital, but essentially peaceful. And *peaceful* had been good. Hadn't it?

CHAPTER SEVEN

GINA was, predictably, on cloud nine at the unexpected turn of events that allowed her to skip her final class, which was maths. She was also, even more predictably, on whatever cloud was higher than cloud nine at the prospect of an afternoon with Riccardo.

Charlotte looked down at the bobbing black head and smiled. It was surprising how readily Gina had welcomed Riccardo into her life. She had been told that he had not been around because of circumstances, but that now he was, and so happy to have her in his life. And with absolute childish trust she had accepted the story. If she had been a couple of years older, Charlotte was sure that the situation would have been very different.

When she started thinking like that, when she witnessed her daughter's excitement and realised how important a figure Riccardo was for her, she couldn't suppress the surge of guilt that overwhelmed her. Who could blame Riccardo for his fury?

He was waiting for them in the taxi, and as soon as they were inside he turned to Gina and asked, smiling, where she would like to go as there was 'some work' being done at the house so they couldn't go back there just yet.

'Work?' Charlotte asked, ears pricking up. 'I hope this doesn't involve any over-the-top presents for Gina...' She had visions of gigantic games consoles and home cinemas crowding the bedroom. Sometimes fathers with limitless supplies of money could be impractical when it came to giving presents to their offspring, and Riccardo, seeing himself as the wounded party who had been denied his child for eight years, might just find himself strolling down that inappropriate route. She would have to nip it in the bud.

'We know, don't we, Gina, that pressies are for special occasions *only*. Birthdays...Christmas...maybe a reward for something out of the ordinary.'

Gina failed to give support to this theory, and Charlotte frowned at her until she said, glumly, 'Yes, Mum.'

'Thoroughly commendable!' Riccardo agreed, and Charlotte looked at him suspiciously. 'It's crazy to buy things for kids just because you can *afford* to! Takes away their motivation to succeed and doesn't teach them how to value money.'

Gina sighed in resignation.

'So if none of that in the house is anything to do with Gina...'

'Oh, but I never said that it had nothing to do with Gina. Look, we're here.' He leant towards his daughter and pointed out of the window as the taxi slowed in front of a very exclusive-looking sports centre. 'Nice swimming pool. How do you fancy a swim?'

'But I didn't bring a swimsuit.'

'With a little luck you can get one inside. It's a small shop but well stocked. Caters for eight-year-old kids who forget to bring their swimsuits.'

'Riccardo…'

'We'll talk in a minute.'

'Okay…' They walked inside the very small, very intimate sports centre where it became immediately apparent that Riccardo was the owner. 'The minute's up. Now, tell me what the heck's happening inside my house while we…while we relax in your private little health spa!' She stood still and folded her arms, refusing to go a step further.

'It's not *my* private little health spa, although I do admit membership is by invitation only.'

'Well…?'

'Well, I would have preferred it to be a surprise, but…guess what?' He looked down at Gina whose ears had pricked up at the word 'surprise'. Then he stooped down to her level, forcing Charlotte to bend down so that she could hear what he had to say, although she was beginning to have an inkling of an idea. 'Your mum's had you all to herself for eight years, and it wasn't her fault, but…' and he took his daughter's hand and covered it with both of his '…now that I'm here, I would very much like to move in so that I can share every day with you.'

Gina beamed and flung her arms around him. Above, he heard a strangulated sound and decided to ignore it. The feeling of his daughter's head pressed into the curve of his neck was answer enough that he had done the right thing.

'Whoa!' Charlotte managed to croak out. 'Stop right there!'

'Mum! I'm going to have my very own dad at home!'

'Gina…' Since Riccardo was showing no signs of standing up, Charlotte reluctantly knelt alongside him, but at an awkward angle because of the narrowness of her skirt. 'I think you'll find that perhaps your *very own dad* hasn't quite thought the matter through.'

'What do you mean, Mum?'

'Maybe we should sit down and discuss this, honey.' The dark brown eyes were beginning to look a little anxious, but Gina nodded and Charlotte led the way, walking briskly over to one of the little circular tables by the bar area. It was comfortable and agreeably empty, just a few businessmen relaxing in the corner, and an elegant foursome of wealthy mummies decked out in very tight designer keep-fit gear. With well-bred good manners, none of them glanced in their direction although they must have been curious.

'I know it would be *super* if Ricc… *Dad* moved in. It's just not possible, as I'm sure he'll agree once he hears me out.'

'Oh.' Gina slumped. 'All my friends have dads.'

'And so do you, honey!'

'Their dads live with them.'

'And, well…' Charlotte cast her mind around wildly for the least aggressive way of saying what she had to say. 'I'm sure your dad would too but he's a *very* important man who has *lots and lots* of big companies, and he just can't run them from a small, tiny house like ours.' She shook her head ruefully and shot Riccardo a look that should have turned him to stone.

Riccardo met her look steadily and mouthed, above

Gina's head, 'Forget it'. Then he smiled down at his daughter. 'Your mum's right about one thing, Gina. I *do* have lots of companies to look after, but that's why we couldn't go back to the house straightaway.'

'Why?'

'Because lots of men are there right now making sure that I have everything I need to work as much as I can from home.'

'What?' The polite groups of people glanced across, and Charlotte modulated her voice to a venomous hiss. 'What?'

'Computer, fax, internet access, the lot,' Riccardo told her coolly.

Between them, Gina could barely contain herself, while Charlotte gritted her teeth and tried not to scream. *How could he?* How could he just think that he could walk through her door and take up residence? But she knew, of course. One reason was Ben, the non-existent fiancé whom Riccardo regarded as a threat, but far weightier than that was his determination to be a full-time father to his child. Lord knew he had no feelings towards *her*, but that, Charlotte realised, would just be a minor sticking point for him. He was Italian, and family was all.

'You can't, Riccardo,' she told him in a sibilant undertone.

'I can and I will and don't even think of stopping me.' He beamed at Gina and pointed to the small, exclusive sportswear shop. 'You run and pick yourself a swimsuit.'

'I'll call the police!'

'And say what—that Gina's father wants to share the

same house as his daughter? That he would even be willing to buy his family as big a house as they want to accommodate his simple wish?'

'Oh *please*! Since when have you *ever* done *anything* that could be classified as *simple*?'

I once loved you. The thought flashed into Riccardo's head and disappeared as quickly as it had come, leaving him momentarily shaken. Then he remembered that those times were gone and, standing in front of him now, she was simply the mother of his child, and moreover the woman who wanted to come between them.

'Don't argue with me, Charlie.'

'You're the most high handed, arrogant, *pig headed* man I have *ever* met in my entire life!'

'I'll take that as a compliment.' He allowed himself a triumphant smile at the notion that Ben the cook would no longer be able to come and go in his daughter's life as he pleased.

'And where do you imagine you're going to sleep?'

'Guest room. To start with.'

'To start with?' Charlotte felt faint.

'I might decide to build an extension, although I have to admit it would be easier all round if we just moved into a bigger house. And you're in the perfect position to find the ideal place. Why don't you consider it a priority? That way I won't get under your feet too much.'

'You...you *can't*.'

Riccardo sighed. 'We're just going over old ground here, Charlie. Why fight the inevitable?' He glanced to where Gina was dangling a swimsuit and gesticulating madly. She wanted them both to swim, and had picked out an especially charming swimsuit for Charlotte in horrible hues of blues and reds which was clearly designed for maximum exposure. Charlotte declined, preferring to watch them both from the sidelines of the pool where she could stew in frustrated silence. Riccardo, she noted sourly, was doing extraordinary things on the bonding front—teaching Gina how to swim breast stroke, tossing her into the air, balancing her on his shoulders so that she could stumble off with squeals of laughter. He didn't look at Charlotte once. But then why should he? she thought. He had got his own way after all.

The whole afternoon, drifting into early evening, was a nightmare. They ate in the restaurant, with Riccardo playing the good dad and compelling her into the role of either *good* mum or utterly miserable sour-faced mum.

By the time they were on their way back to the house, Charlotte's face ached from the strain of having to pretend.

But as promised the work was done, everything tidied up, by his personal assistant, she'd been told while they'd been at the club 'having fun'. And Gina was exhausted. Too tired for anything more than her nightie and half a story.

Which just left them and a quiet house.

'You'll need a towel,' she said wearily, sinking into a chair in the sitting room, all the better to contemplate the unravelling of her life. 'Lord, Riccardo, I can't believe you've done this.' She rubbed her eyes with her thumbs and then closed them.

'So, why don't you try making the most of it?'

Charlotte opened her eyes to him sitting on the arm

of her chair, but she was just too tired to respond to the invasion of privacy. 'How? We don't like each other, and yet I'm supposed to be happy sharing my space with you.'

For some reason, that hurt him. He stood up and walked towards the door, pausing to glance at her over his shoulder. 'Well, if it's any consolation, my routine at my office will continue as usual, and yes, I'll be around in the evenings, but if this arrangement really doesn't work out then we'll reconsider the whole thing.'

'Meaning what?'

Riccardo shrugged. 'Meaning we'll do the amicable joint-custody thing and I'll just have to reconcile myself to not being around in a full-time capacity.'

'You should have thought of that before you embarked on this crazy moving in idea!'

'I'm going to have a shower. If you need me I'll be working at the desk in my bedroom.'

He shut the door quietly behind him, leaving Charlotte a little disappointed that the argument she was fired up to conduct had fizzled out like a damp squib. But at least he had agreed to clear off if things didn't work out. Which, naturally, they wouldn't. Any fool would have predicted *that*. He didn't like her and she didn't like him. There was just too much water under the bridge, whether he wanted to admit it or not.

Except…except…

There had been moments at that wretched spa when she had forgotten her anger and experienced a little taste of family life, ordinary family life with laughter and teasing and *fun*, and someone else there sharing the little things. The frightening thing was that it could get to be a habit, but…

She stood up and headed up the stairs. It was a small house. Just the three bedrooms and a shared bathroom—and he wasn't in it. There was no sound of running water and there was a crack of light under his bedroom door. At least for the time being she would have to get used to this inconvenience. She grabbed her clothes from her room and, head still full of ridiculous but tantalising thoughts, she gave a brief knock on the bathroom door and opened it.

Riccardo, naked and shaving in front of the bathroom-cabinet mirror, saw her enter and freeze. He rinsed his face and turned around.

'What's the problem? You've seen this body naked before.'

Charlotte, clutching her bundle of clothes for dear life, glued her eyes to his face. That was safe. And right now she needed that safe haven because her legs had turned to lead.

'Argh…'

'Did you want to use the bathroom?' He strolled towards her. Eight years on and she still blushed like a virgin. He had been out with women who were willing to do the most explicit things and had never turned a hair, never mind looked as though they wanted the ground to open up and swallow them.

'Ah…umm…'

'What is it about me that you don't like?' That passing remark had been niggling away at him like a thorn in his side. Resentment and even hatred he could deal with, because he could tie them up to a reaction to how they had parted company, and whether or not he agreed with it he could now understand it. But just *not liking* him was a bit more difficult to get his head around. He knew that physically he could still affect her. Experience with the opposite sex had made him a master in reading their responses. But just not liking him implied something that bordered on emotional indifference, and for the first time in his life the physical was just not good enough. He wanted more from her, and he told himself that that was because their situation was so complicated.

Charlotte made an inarticulate sound and began feeling for the door behind her.

'No, no. Not so fast.' Physically, he had to admit, *she* certainly still affected *him*, evidence of which was all too visible should she allow her eyes to travel due south. He snatched his towel from where he had draped it over the shower rail and slung it around his waist. 'There. Better?'

'I'm not having a conversation with you in here!'

'Why not? It's as good a place as any.'

'It's a bathroom!'

'Since when did you become so conventional, Charlie? If I recall, you never allowed inappropriate locations to get in the way of what you wanted to do.' He leaned against the door, effectively locking her in.

'I don't *want* to talk to you, though, Riccardo. I *want* to have a bath.'

'Feel free.'

'This is *my* house.' She tilted her head up mutinously and swallowed down the unsettling feeling in her stomach as she stared into his eyes, feeling a bit like plummeting sharply and unexpectedly down on a rollercoaster ride. 'You may have taken it upon yourself to move in *temporarily*, because you just can't *bear* not to get your own way, but you're still under *my* roof, and just so long as you are I won't have you disrupting my life and what I want to do!'

'This isn't a question about me!'

'Yes, it is!' His bare torso was only inches away from her and she could feel her body prickling with awareness. It was unbearable, especially as she knew he was aroused. How could she not? She might have kept her eyes plastered on his face, but she still hadn't been able to miss his very obvious erection. She told herself that that meant nothing. She had fallen in love with a man who was capable of conducting a relationship based solely on sex. She just wasn't going there again.

Nevertheless, her breasts ached; every part of her ached.

'It's about us trying to make something work for the sake of someone else. Gina didn't ask to be born into a single-parent family, and I'm giving us both the chance to try and do something about it.'

'Okay. But can we discuss this somewhere else? Because…'

'Because you're really desperate for a bath? Because you call yourself *Charlotte* now and have an overdeveloped puritan streak? Or maybe it's because you're terrified I might do *this*…'

He leaned down into her and kissed her. No gentle, explorative kiss, but a kiss that was fiercely, urgently hungry, pinning her back against the door.

Charlotte could feel his hardness pressed against her, and with a stifled moan of desperation she went under.

Of their own volition, her hands reached up and her fingers curled into his still-damp hair, and when he flattened his hand in the small of her back and pulled her into him she didn't resist. She just couldn't. It was as if she had been waiting eight years for this moment to happen and now that it had she was powerless to do anything about it.

His tongue was in her mouth, probing and demanding, and when he stopped kissing her it was so that he could do more, reach for the buttons on the snappy no-nonsense blouse she was still wearing, and begin unfastening them one by one. And not nearly fast enough. She helped him, shakily undoing the last, and drowning in a sea of pleasure as he pulled open the blouse, exposing her lacy white bra. Without pausing, he slipped his finger into her cleavage and stroked the sensitive skin between her breasts.

For Charlotte, nothing had ever felt so good. But then, no one had touched her since him. Those familiar hands were like heaven. He pushed down the lacy cups and her breasts spilled out, succulent, plump fruit waiting to be tasted.

Riccardo, always in control of his body, had to steady himself to avoid the unthinkable happening. He had no idea how they had moved so swiftly to this point, but at this very moment eight years had never elapsed. She was all his as she'd been back then. Her nipples were big and defined and rosy with arousal. He teased their erect peaks with his fingers, enjoying those little noises of pleasure she made, and then he sank to his knees so that he could take them into his mouth, licking, sucking, nipping them with his teeth, until he could feel her wanting to cry out but restraining herself.

When he tugged the bra off her breasts bounced free, and he cupped them in his hands and massaged them, while he continued his exploration of her body, first trailing his mouth against her flat stomach, then squatting so that he could ease off the remainder of her clothes, and she helped, stepping out of them, eager to have no barriers between their naked bodies. He blew gently on the soft curls that guarded her most intimate place.

Her fingers were resting lightly on his head, but at that they curled into his hair. When he raised his eyes, he saw that she was arched back, her eyes shut, her breathing quick and shallow.

He dipped into her moist femininity and tasted her, a slow and lingering taste that made her quiver and wriggle against his mouth. With remembered enjoyment, she began to move rhythmically against him, a soft up-and-down slide as he took her higher and higher. His tongue flicked and slid and teased the throbbing bud, but it was only when he stood up, ready to hoist her onto him, that Charlotte opened her eyes and the full reality of her situation sank in.

'We...we can't, Riccardo.'

'Don't even think of stopping this now.' Riccardo growled his answer.

'This is what got us into the situation we're in now...unprotected sex.'

And so what if it happens again? The thought

slammed into Riccardo like a closed fist, almost making him reel backwards from the silent admission. He put that disturbing thought on hold and snatched the discarded towel back up. 'Then we'll make sure we use protection.'

'I haven't got any!'

Which raised another question, but that too he put on hold. His body was on fire and he *had* to have her.

'Leave it to me.'

Charlotte struggled to feel some healthy disgust at a man who travelled with a portable supply of contraception, but she was burning up. In those few seconds, as she tried to snap out of her crazy trance, Riccardo manoeuvred her aside and opened the door, while she flung back on her clothes in a haphazard fashion, not bothering to button or zip anything up. Then to his room, the little guest room at the far end of the landing.

'Gina…'

'Will be fine.' He locked the bedroom door, and at the sound of the key turning she felt a thrill of heady, forbidden excitement. She was also in the grip of a 'what the heck' reckless urge. She was violently attracted to this man and it had never stopped, not even when he'd no longer been around and her only bed companions had been bitterness and disillusionment. It was as if her body obeyed a different set of rules to her head.

He didn't switch the light on nor did he close the curtains, and in the silvery darkness she was mesmerised by the sight of his naked, muscular body.

She automatically stripped off her top. The bra she had left discarded on the bathroom floor. Then she stepped out of the rest of her clothes so that they were both standing only feet apart, eyes locked. Riccardo was the first to break their mutual appraisal by holding out his hand to lead her to the bed. It was a single bed, and hardly ideal, but to Charlotte it might well have been the most romantic venue in the world.

'Well, now,' Riccardo murmured. 'Shall we take up where we left off?'

'This is absolute madness.' But there was a smile in her voice that made his heart sing.

'What's the point of life if we don't succumb to a little healthy madness once in a while? Now, where were we?'

'You were…'

'Yes?'

'I see you're still the tease in bed you always were…' Charlotte murmured, guiding his hand to where she still ached for his touch.

'Only with you,' Riccardo said huskily. He was relieved that she didn't ask him to explain that, because he had no idea what he had meant or even how he had managed to utter the words, but he had meant them. *Crazy.*

He made love to her slowly and sweetly, touching every inch of her body, and the more he touched, the more he remembered, almost as if the image of her had been lying somewhere just below the surface. He even remembered the way she moved and sighed, and all the little noises she made to express her pleasure.

'So,' he said afterwards, when they were lying interlocked on the single bed. 'Tell me you can't make a go of this, Charlie.'

'I give up trying to get you to call me *Charlotte*.'

Riccardo stroked some blonde hair back and kissed her nose. 'Somehow *Charlotte* seems too proper. We're good together.'

'We're good *in bed* together,' Charlotte said on a sigh. 'And I still have a bath to run.'

'It can wait.'

'For what? Nothing's changed, Riccardo.'

'We just made love!' He pulled her against him, because he could feel her shifting to get out of the bed. 'Did you?'

'Did I what?'

'Touch him. Make love to him.' He had to know, and this went far beyond simple curiosity.

'Don't bring Ben into this.'

'Did you? Forget it. Forget I ever asked.' He sprawled onto his back and stared upwards at the ceiling. 'Go have your bath, Charlie. You're right. Nothing's changed.'

'Okay. No. No, I didn't. It wasn't that type of relationship.'

'What type is that?' Riccardo addressed the ceiling, but suddenly he felt on top of the world. So he had been right all along—it had been a passion-free zone! Maybe a kiss or two, a friendly peck on the cheek, he liked to think, and he could deal with that. He didn't know where this fierce possessiveness had come from, but he wasn't going to rail against it. She was the mother of his child and he was an Italian man. It was understandable.

'I told you. After what happened between us, I had a big rethink on what I wanted out of a relationship and I knew that it wasn't just sex. It didn't matter how good the sex was, in the end it just never counts for very much.'

As swiftly as he had hit the top of the world, he

plummeted back down to earth and straight back into the brick wall of her *not liking* him. He knew he should rise above this. Damn it, it was hardly as though he hadn't enjoyed women, having made sure that they knew in advance that he was only interested in relationships that came without strings. He was no saint, but he felt as if she was enclosed within four ice walls. And she didn't want to bring the paragon *Ben* into the conversation because she still needed him.

'Look.' She stepped out of the bed and began putting on her clothes, glad for the distraction of doing something rather than lying there next to the man she now, with gut-wrenching dismay, realised she still loved. 'I'm prepared to put Gina ahead of myself and let you stay here, at least for a while, until she gets to know you and feels safe enough to let you move out without thinking that you'll disappear for ever. But there's one big condition.'

And he would never know how important the condition was for her health, because sleeping with him had been a crazy mistake and she couldn't do it again. It would be bad enough having him in the house, but to start having a sexual relationship with him again would spell a honeyed trap which she couldn't fall into again.

'We don't do this again.' Clothes on, she looked at him sprawled on the bed, half covered with the tousled bed clothes that were a mocking reminder of her weakness. She took a deep breath. 'It was a mistake, and I guess it was a mistake we both had to make, but the same old same old doesn't work for me any more.'

'Same old same old?'

Charlotte shrugged. 'Same old Riccardo, the good lover with nothing more on his mind.'

'I proposed marriage!' Riccardo reminded her, enraged at his impotence, at her for her moral high-ground, and at his own confusion because the thought of her and her sensitive twenty-first-century wimp stirred hot, ugly jealousy inside him.

But where's the love? she asked herself sadly. 'You just don't understand, Riccardo. Anyway. That's not important. I'm going to have my bath, and like I said we'll both put Gina first and see how it goes for a little while.' She didn't trust herself with him. He could manoeuvre a conversation in directions she didn't know existed until she found herself going down one of them, and she couldn't let herself be persuaded into a relationship with him on his terms. So she opened the door and, before he could say anything else, she let herself quietly out of the room and straight to the bathroom.

Not important? *Not important?* Riccardo, staring in frustration at the closed door, was outraged. What, he thought venomously, did that man have that *he* didn't? And how could she just write off physical attraction as something that didn't count for *anything*? Moreover, would she still be able to have a relationship with the man after she had slept with *him*? He could have kicked himself for not asking her that vital question, and then it occurred to him that maybe, in the great scheme of things, he was emotionally so unimportant that their one-night *mistake* wouldn't even register.

But he was finding he damned well *wanted* it to register! He had been young and arrogant and had let her go, thinking that it was the best for the both of them. He was beginning to wonder whether that had been a mistake from which he had never really recovered. But fate had given him this second chance. He wasn't going to make the same mistake twice, not when there was so much at stake.

CHAPTER EIGHT

'WHAT'S going on?' Charlotte stepped through her front door at a little after seven-thirty, to find Riccardo right there and apparently waiting for her. This was disconcerting. In fact, the past two-and-a-half weeks had been disconcerting. She could accuse him of a lot of things, but not making an effort for the sake of his daughter was not one of them. How long he could keep it up was anybody's guess, but if the object of the exercise was to get close to his daughter then he was succeeding with flying colours.

He'd been getting back to the house by seven. He had taken Gina to the cinema twice to see shows which she couldn't imagine he'd enjoyed in a month of Sundays. He had endured a Saturday evening meal in a fast-food restaurant surrounded by babies, toddlers, young children running about and harassed mothers without complaint. He had played Scrabble and contrived to lose, Monopoly—which he hadn't quite been able to bring himself to lose—and endless games of cards which Charlotte could only think he'd found supremely tiresome compared to his previous adult pursuits. On a scale of one to ten, where, she wondered, did gin rummy figure compared to a Friday evening in the company of one of his leggy blondes at a posh restaurant?

Charlotte had watched from a distance, joining in when she had to, but protecting herself from seeing all this effort as anything more than Riccardo approaching a situation with the one hundred percent desire to succeed with which he approached all situations.

Aside from her. Because he'd assiduously left her alone. He'd laughed, he'd joked, but his attention had been primarily for his daughter. There had not been the slightest hint that anything physical had taken place between them. He had been, she was forced to admit, the perfect gentleman. The cynical side of her couldn't help but think that he was covering ground quickly with Gina so that he could clear out of the house, having realised that sex with her mother was no longer an option.

'Food,' Riccardo said succinctly. He began helping her out of her coat while Charlotte, bewildered, wondered what he was on about.

'You're wearing my apron.'

'Well spotted.'

'It looks ridiculous.' But she had to smile. Riccardo, decked out in old chinos, a tee-shirt and sporting an apron bought by Gina that declared the joys of motherhood, was priceless. 'I wish I had a camera,' she said. 'This is a moment worth capturing.'

'Go upstairs and have a bath.'

'Yes, but...'

'Gina's with one of her school friends. Last-minute thing. Going to the movies, so she won't be back home until about eight-thirty. I thought that would be all right as tomorrow's Saturday.'

'Well...' Charlotte felt a little twinge of alarm. Gina had been their chaperone for the past couple of weeks, always around with them both and filling in potentially awkward silences with relentless chatter. When she hadn't been around, Riccardo had disappeared to work and Charlotte had curled up in front of the television, always making sure to take a handy book to duck behind should he appear without warning.

'It's a good opportunity to discuss...domestic arrangements,' Riccardo said vaguely.

'Oh. Right.' So *that* was what he was up to! Now would come the nitty-gritty details of when he would leave the house. Charlotte felt it in her bones, and knew that she should have been over the moon because her life would get back to normal, but she felt an empty void settle in the pit of her stomach.

Why fight the truth? She had become accustomed to having him around the house. She had always thought that two was such a tidy number. Just her and Gina, both of them against the world. But three was just so much *rounder* and more fulfilling.

If he thought that cooking a meal was the adult, civilised way of breaking the news, then she would show him that she was fine with that idea and dress accordingly, in her usual casual, staying at home 'because I love my life without you in it' gear—a pair of comfy combat trousers, and a baggy olive-green sweater.

She was not expecting what she found in the kitchen.

Candlelight, for a start. Riccardo turned around as she walked in, and Charlotte smiled awkwardly at him.

'I didn't dress for the occasion.' She spread her hands along her randomly put together outfit, feeling a bit of a fool even though he was in casual clothes as well. Though somehow he looked considerably less scruffy than she was.

'No matter.'

'You've cooked a meal from *scratch*?' She spotted the recipe book propped against the bread bin and the sink full of pots and pans, which seemed to suggest an awfully ambitious meal just for two. Why did he have to get under her skin like that? Why did he have to make her *like* him?

'There's no need to sound quite so astounded,' Riccardo said. He fetched something from the fridge. It turned out to be avocado and prawns.

'I thought you hated cooking, and sneered at men who ventured anywhere near a kitchen unless in pursuit of a bottle of wine from the fridge.' She sat down and tried to squash the foolishly special feeling rushing through her. This just wasn't going to do, was it?

'Obviously I wouldn't make it my life's work.' He handed her the dish, the avocado and prawns both drowning under ample amounts of seafood sauce, which he had bought because the recipe had seemed ridiculously long considering the length of time that would be spent eating the damned thing. 'It might taste better than it looks,' he said, picking up his fork and diving into the starter. 'Not bad.' Fairly revolting. Ben the Chef probably did all manner of creative things involving herbs and spices, which immediately made Riccardo scowl.

'It's not that bad,' Charlotte told him, misinterpreting his expression.

Riccardo grunted. Most evenings she worked long hours. Way too long. Never mind that she had an excellent childminder. It had crossed his mind more than once that she'd need not necessarily been at work, that she could have been seeing her boyfriend behind his back. It had crossed his mind even more that he could have her followed and put his suspicions to rest once and for all, but he'd baulked at the idea. He didn't want to discover whether she had broken ties with Ben or not; he didn't want to have to deal with the confrontation that would result from such a discovery. Because it had become blatantly clear to him over the past couple of weeks that he wanted her in his life. He had no idea how he could have been so stupid as to think that the physical spark between them would be enough to cement the union he felt his daughter deserved. Charlotte might have caved in once, but she had made it perfectly clear as time had gone by that that had really meant as little to her as she had told him at the time.

Riccardo, always at the top of the game when it came to women, had felt for the first time in his life superfluous to requirements. His presence was tolerated because he had inflicted it upon her, leaving her no option but to concede temporary defeat. But he could sense her waiting for him to leave. It enraged and frustrated him at the same time.

'What's that?' He realised that she had been talking to him, making polite conversation the way you would with a stranger.

'I wondered when was the last time you cooked anything.'

'Is that a comment on the food?' he asked, still scowling, and standing up to clear away the dishes.

'No, of course not!' Charlotte protested, taken aback. 'I was just making polite conversation.'

As he had thought. 'Strangers make polite conversation.' He tried to keep his voice level and jovial. 'Usually people who have a child in common can be a bit more relaxed with one another.'

Charlotte refrained from pointing out that most people who had a child in common probably had a more conventional union. Instead she asked him brightly what he had cooked.

'Pasta.'

'Yummy. Italian food. My favourite.'

'I know.' *Steer away from confrontation.* 'Although…' he drained some tagliatelle and noted that it looked a bit on the tough side, hopefully convincingly *al dente* '…I can't guarantee it'll taste like anything you ever had in Italy.'

'Smells good, though.' This was bliss. Back from work, the smell of food in the kitchen, Riccardo busying himself… When she had invented Ben as her fiancé with a magical culinary touch, she had had no idea just how wonderful the 'man in kitchen' package could be. Thus far, she and Riccardo had avoided eating together. She had grabbed a sandwich and so had he, at a different time in the evening, and then there had been the occasional father and daughter bonding visits to a couple of local fast-food places. On weekends, admittedly, meals had been shared, but with Gina sitting solidly between them.

This situation now took domesticity onto a different and dangerous level.

Charlotte, waiting for the verbal knife to fall, decided that she would initiate the first cut. Attack was always going to be better than defence, she reckoned. Better to be empowered than reduced to being told that, yes, he would be on his way now, and thank heavens they hadn't done anything crazy like get married.

It was clear that he was on edge. In fact, as she tried to chat about the food—asking him all sorts of questions about ingredients and cooking times, while she frantically tried to work out how she could manoeuvre the conversation skilfully into the place she wanted—she noticed that he was all but gritting his teeth together.

'I'll have to try this one,' she said in a cheery voice.

'Will you?' He looked at her narrowly, wondering whether that meant that the boyfriend had been sidelined.

'Sure! I mean, it's not as though you're going to be around here for ever, whipping up mushrooms and tomatoes and tagliatelle for my benefit!' There. It was out in the open, and Charlotte was quietly relieved to have taken the bull by the horns. She stared at herself twirling pasta round and round her fork, and felt sickeningly oppressed by the knowledge that he was staring at her and thinking…*what*? Thanking God she'd broken the ice on a difficult subject? Hoping she hadn't started thinking it was going to be permanent? Thinking that he'd never thought she led such a boring life, watching television and reading books every evening, or that he'd never imagined she possessed so many dreary clothes?

Riccardo watched her downbent head and stilled. 'Right. I wasn't actually going to bring up this subject just at the moment...'

'I know. We should maybe wait until we finish eating, but why not just get it over with and discussed? You're on edge, I'm on edge. You're right about us not being strangers, so why should we beat about the bush when it comes to discussing something as important as this?' Charlotte was rapidly going off her food. 'I was horrified when you moved yourself into my house, but I have to admit that the experiment worked much better than I thought it was going to.'

'The experiment?'

'Yes.' She rather liked the sound of that word: *experiment*. It sort of removed her from being personally involved, turned them all into little white mice scurrying round and round in a cage. Little white mice didn't fall victim to broken hearts. 'Face it, Riccardo, you might think you know it all, but—'

'Hang on a minute!' He slammed his fist on the table. 'Why don't you climb down from your perfect pedestal for a minute and stop the categorizing?'

'I wasn't categorizing.'

'No? Then why do you imagine that I think I *know it all*? Would that be because I'm still the bastard who turned his back eight years ago? It's a damned long time to be still affected by the past, Charlie! Anyone would think that there's a reason for that.'

'A reason? What kind of reason?'

'So what sort of timescale do you have in mind here?'

Just at that moment, washing the dishes seemed a very good idea. He took her plate, impatiently ordering her to stay put when she offered to help with the tidying, at which she subsided into a series of polite utterances: 'Are you sure?' and 'Okay, if you insist.' Riccardo felt his mood drop another couple of notches from foul to downright filthy.

Now for the first time he could see that there would be no point to his staying under her roof. She had been right after all. An unnatural relationship for the sake of a child would have been all wrong, and sooner or later Gina would have been affected by it, far more so than if they did the inevitable now and went their separate ways.

He would not debate her decision. Pride slammed into place and settled over him like an ice-cold shroud.

'Well, I think we can both agree that you're doing an amazing job bonding with Gina.'

'And you thought that I wouldn't?' Riccardo asked coldly, his back to her as he ploughed into the dishes with the speed of someone vastly unconcerned about grease remnants.

'No! I just thought…' She might have spent the past two-and-a-half weeks watching far too much television and lurking behind books in an attempt to avoid him, but she would miss the way her heart fluttered whenever he was around, miss the way he interacted with Gina, making her smile and just being there to pick up the slack when Charlotte had been feeling exhausted. She would even miss the way they sometimes sided against her when she began giving one of her speeches about nutrition. Tears threatened, and she swallowed them back. 'I thought you might have found it difficult to bond at first. I mean, it's not as though you have a lot of experience with children.'

'She's an easy child. Intelligent. Outgoing. Outspoken.' He ran water over a plate and slung it on the draining board, where it balanced precariously against a frying pan.

'Yes. And I'm really pleased that things worked out… Well on that front. I suppose she's at the perfect age—curious, willing to give people and situations the benefit of the doubt.' When she closed her eyes, she could relive the sight of him naked, his broad shoulders and athletic, muscular frame glistening with perspiration as he drove deep into her. She cleared her throat to dispel the burgeoning image. 'But of course, that's only part of the big picture, which is why I accept that this living arrangement has to come to an end. As far as timescale goes, well, I guess you'd agree that sooner is better than later. I mean, I know it's going to be hard for Gina, because you've been on the scene for over two weeks now, but I think that you're well bonded enough with her that she can feel secure in the knowledge that even when you go she'll carry on seeing you.'

The last of the dishes now completed the pyramid which threatened to topple over, and Charlotte stood up and fetched a tea towel from the drawer. 'I can tell you don't do much washing up, Riccardo,' she joked, to distract herself from the hollowness of the reality opening up in front of her. She picked up a plate from the top and dried it, feeling his proximity like a knife wound.

Riccardo thought that that was typical, because despite all her chat about his great bonding talents—as though connecting with his own flesh and blood had really been some kind of mountain he had been obliged to try and climb—she still saw him as essentially the arrogant bastard who had rejected her once upon a time. She hadn't let it go in eight years and she never would.

'Well, no.' Riccardo shrugged one of those dismissive shrugs that spoke volumes of the man who ran an empire with a steel fist. Pride would not allow him to plead his case. If she'd dismissed him as a bastard, then why fight the image? 'Why should I?'

He stood back from her and folded his arms. From a detached point of view, he disapproved thoroughly of what she was wearing. Combat trousers and sloppy cotton jumpers that looked as though they had been through the wash a thousand times were not, in his opinion, the kind of sexy, feminine gear he liked to see women in. But oddly, over the past couple of weeks, he had grown accustomed to her curled up in her comfy clothes, and it now struck him that he, too, had begun to dress down. It wasn't surprising, really, considering how casual life was in her house. It wasn't a place fashioned for designer clothes. That he had changed without even noticing it jarred.

'Limitless money can buy limitless things,' he heard himself say, and winced internally at the high-handed bore he sounded. 'Including a dishwasher. Not, of course, that I usually find myself facing stacks of dirty dishes. Isn't that what good restaurants are for?'

'I find it more fun to do the washing up with Gina

by hand,' Charlotte said coolly. 'It's a nice time for us to catch up and chat. But I guess in the world you live in catching up at the end of the day at the kitchen sink just isn't *quite* the done thing. Anyway, who would you have to catch up with?'

She closed the cupboard door on the last of the dried dishes and retreated to the safety of the kitchen chair. It felt good to argue with him. Really, if she was going to say goodbye, then she couldn't face saying goodbye to a considerate, witty, sexy, 'cooking a meal and doing the dishes' Riccardo. She drew her legs up and propped her chin on her knees. When she glanced down, she could see her perfectly painted pink toenails. She had given herself a pedicure two days ago. It was something she never did, but Riccardo had been downstairs explaining fractions to Gina, and she had found herself in the wonderful and novel situation of being able to spend a little quality time on herself. So she had painted her toenails.

Afterwards, she had realised that a part of her had done it for his benefit. He liked women who had painted toenails. It was something he had told her years ago in passing. Not, she knew, that he would even spare a glance at *hers*, but she had done it anyway. Just looking at them now made her angry with herself because she had disobeyed all her own rules of self-preservation and allowed herself to fall in love with him all over again.

She looked at him standing there, tea towel slung carelessly over one shoulder, arms folded as he stared right back at her.

'Meaning *what* exactly?' Riccardo asked tightly.

'Meaning that you haven't exactly spent the past

eight years committing yourself to another human being, have you, Riccardo? No long-term partner, no family. Just a series of *babes*, and everyone knows that men don't catch up with *babes* over the kitchen sink. Men catch up with them over some Chablis and French food in a restaurant, followed by a hot night in the sack. I'll bet you've never even gone on holiday with any of them!' Okay, she was pushing it, she could tell by the grim, shuttered expression on his face, but perversely that made her feel good.

No, he hadn't. Many had hinted, but he wouldn't have dreamt of doing any such thing.

Riccardo pushed himself away from the kitchen counter against which he had been leaning and strode towards the door. 'A little childish all this, isn't it, Charlie?' He paused and looked down at her coldly. 'Hurling insults. When we should be discussing the next step forward like civilised adults. I'm going into the sitting room where we can talk in comfort. Follow me, but if you don't I feel I should warn you that I'll have no alternative but to get lawyers involved. I want firm visiting rights, and if you can't control yourself when you're with me then it's a pretty good indicator that you'll be impetuous and unreliable when it comes to any situation we agree informally.'

Charlotte flushed, stood up and followed him, feeling ashamed of her outburst. 'I'm sorry,' was the first thing she said as soon as they had sat down, facing one another. 'You're right. I shouldn't have commented on your personal life. I was out of order.'

'I can be out of here by tomorrow evening,' Riccardo

told her bluntly, ignoring the apology. 'I'll want to spend it with Gina, as you might understand.'

''Course.' Winter would roll into spring, then into summer, and on and on and on. She wondered how she would feel as time went by and she saw him every week, twice a week, how ever many times, there at her house, collecting their daughter. She wondered how she would feel when there was a woman's face looking out from the passenger seat of his car. 'But when it comes to these arrangements there are a few conditions.'

'Yes?'

'Gina can't be out too late during the week because of her homework. So on the agreed days you'll have to arrange to be here fairly early so that she can be brought back home by, let's say, eight-thirty. That would give her time to do some homework and have a bath before you come so that she can just hop into bed when you drop her off.'

'Fine. But you'll have to understand that I work, and I can't always plan meetings down to a certain hour. Sometimes I'll have to give you very short notice of when I can see her, but I guarantee it'll be no less than twice a week, and I want her every other weekend.'

'She's going to be pulled from pillar to post,' Charlotte whispered, on the verge of tears.

'I gave you the option of making our arrangement permanent. You rejected it.'

'For all the right reasons!'

'Then there's the question of holidays.'

'I can't think about that right now.'

'Try,' Riccardo rasped harshly. He watched as she curled herself into a tighter ball on the chair.

'I don't know.'

'I will want her to spend some time in Italy. She has relatives over there, people she's never met.'

'I hadn't thought… How are they going to react?'

'With great joy,' Riccardo said dryly. 'My mother's been after this result for years. 'Course, she would have preferred to have seen her grandchild through the more conventional route of marriage, but there you go.'

'Marriage to a girl with the right connections,' Charlotte said bitterly.

'She gave up on that ambition a long time ago,' Riccardo told her shortly. She had resigned herself to a son who went out with 'babes', none of whom she had ever met anyway because they weren't of the variety that he took on holiday. *Like Charlie had said, with bullseye accuracy.*

'And what about the rest of the world?'

'I'm not following you.'

'Your friends. Business colleagues.'

'What about them?'

'What will they say? What will they think of you? I mean, it's not every day that a big cheese finds himself embroiled in a scandal…'

'Now who's the dinosaur?' Riccardo commented wryly. 'For starters, it's not a scandal. And then gossip involving businessmen barely qualifies as gossip. Anyway…' he shrugged, '…I really don't give a damn about what other people think of the happenings in my personal life.'

Charlotte wished she possessed such insouciance. She might just have been able to deal with Riccardo's presence in her life a bit better. As it was, she had only just recovered from the curiosity of friends and work-mates, who all now knew about Riccardo, and she foresaw miserable times ahead trying to handle her broken life. Which brought her back to her original remark about conditions.

'I also would rather you kept your private life out of Gina's domain…' she said tentatively, and Riccardo frowned. 'I mean…' She continued hurriedly, just in case he thought that she was trying to angle the conversation back to an argument about the women he dated. 'I don't care what you get up to between the sheets, but I don't want Gina being introduced to a procession of your women.'

'And if it's just the one?'

'Well, that would be different. Of course.' *Was there one?* she wondered?

'And should I bring her round for your inspection beforehand? Just to make sure that I'm not contravening any of your moral laws?'

'There's no need to be sarcastic,' Charlotte said hotly.

She looked so *young*. Young and vulnerable, leaning forward in the chair with her feet tucked solidly underneath her as if anchoring them down just in case they decided to stand up and flee. 'No, there's no need. You have my word. The only woman I will ever introduce to Gina will be the woman I intend to commit my life to.'

Charlotte felt a sharp pang at this imaginary woman and nodded.

'I needn't ask a similar condition of you,' Riccardo said politely through gritted teeth. 'As I know there already is a man in your life.' Something felt as though it was being ripped out of him. 'You never said…does Gina get along with him?' God knew, the paragon of a boyfriend, who had been lurking in the background for the past couple of weeks, was probably a dab hand at entertaining eight-year-old children. But no longer could he lay down laws about *her* private life. She had no objection to Gina meeting a woman if he was in a committed relationship. He was obliged to return the favour. More so, considering Gina doubtless had an easy relationship with Ben.

'Oh, most people get along with Ben,' Charlotte said, skirting round the question. 'I'm glad we sorted that one out, Riccardo, although I feel badly that you wasted all that money setting up stuff to work at home.'

'We'll sort out finances another day,' Riccardo said brusquely. He looked at his watch. Gina would be getting back to the house at any minute. 'And I suggest we both sit Gina down and break this to her.'

'Of course.' She hadn't missed that quick glance at his watch. The conversation for him was now terminated. They would provide a united front when they spoke to Gina later, but as far as he was concerned he was through with playing house. He had probably been through with it long before his departure meal tonight. She just hadn't been quick enough to spot it, but then love was good at blurring the focus.

She'd thought that she would be the one reassuring Gina that her dad would still be around even if he would no longer be living under the same roof as they were but, in the end, it was Riccardo who did all the talking. This was the tender side to him she had witnessed over the past weeks in his relationship with his daughter. There was no escaping his devotion, and Gina, instinctively, must have recognised that and believed him implicitly when he told her that he was going to see her as often as he possibly could, at least twice a week.

It was so hard to think that this was the same man who could be so cold and hostile when it suited him.

Later, with Gina in bed, the cold, hostile stranger returned. He would get his lawyer to clarify financial arrangements, he informed her, and he wanted guarantees that her volatile mood swings wouldn't influence his agreed visiting rights.

She looked terrified, curled up on the chair while he towered above her, but it didn't suit Riccardo to lessen the impact of his forceful personality. If anything, he wanted her to know that he would do whatever it took to assume his parental rights, just in case she got it into her head that he might disappear into the background at some convenient point in the future.

'And just to warn you,' he said, walking towards the bay window and perching. 'Expect a little disruption in your life. Up until now, I've kept this situation to myself, but that's over.'

'Disruption?' Charlotte asked, bewildered. 'What are you talking about?'

'Reporters. For Gina's sake, I'll try and keep them off your back, but I'm high profile in the world of business. This unusual situation is bound to generate some interest. So…' He walked towards the door and she followed his leisurely progress across the room warily. 'No men. There's a thin line between reporting and scandal.'

'I thought you didn't *care* about what other people thought of you, Riccardo!' Charlotte said, stung by his implication that she couldn't wait to jump into a relationship the minute he walked out of the front door.

'*I* don't.' He paused, and in his next sentence he managed to tell her exactly what he thought of her. 'But Gina might find it very confusing. And she *is* the important one in the equation, isn't she?'

CHAPTER NINE

CHARLOTTE'S only brush with the press had been a year and a half ago in an article in the local newspaper about the estate agency's expansion into the Midlands market. It had been tucked away on one of the middle pages, where space was given to heart-warming anecdotes and readers' views, under the corny heading of: AND NOW ON A LIGHTER NOTE! The reporter in question had been a bright-eyed and bushy-tailed school leaver who had anxiously consulted her list of questions and written a flattering report about the dynamic young executive who still managed to be a super-mum. Instead of focusing on interest rates, difficult first-time buyer markets or the surge away from London to cheaper outlying districts, she had concentrated on the feminist angle of the woman who could have it all. Frankly, Charlotte had not recognised herself in the descriptions.

She supposed that this was what happened to the bright-eyed and bushy-tailed local reporters—they hit the big time, went to work on national newspapers and mutated into sharks that could scent blood from fifty paces away.

They had homed in on the lucrative theme of 'billionaire with a past', and a shady one at that. She had nothing to say on the subject whenever the phone rang, and least of all when she was confronted with any of them invading her private space. But she seemed to have emerged from the whole saga as a sex siren with an agenda, though how they had arrived at that conclusion she had no idea, considering she hadn't asked him for a penny in all the time she had been a single mother. It was a question she hadn't put to them, too concerned to protect Gina from the invasive publicity, and too harassed from fending off the sudden surge of interest everyone seemed to be taking in her, from close friends to nodding acquaintances. She had fielded enough words of advice to fill an encyclopaedia.

Now, with the minutes ticking past, she peered through the window and spotted two reporters skulking. Next to her, Gina was itching to be off to school. It was Victorian Children Day for the Year Fours. Gina had woken up especially early, thrilled to be heading to school dressed as a ragamuffin Victorian schoolboy with ripped shirt, waistcoat, tattered trousers held up by a piece of corded rope, and school shoes which had been specially scuffed for the purpose. Right now she was content to accept the fact that they would be leaving 'in a minute'. Charlotte knew her daughter well enough to realise that her acceptably impatient shifting from foot to foot would quickly degenerate into querulous whining.

'Oh, come on,' she said, making her mind up. 'We might as well head off.'

'Just tell them to go away, Mum!'

'I would if I thought they'd listen.'

'Then get Dad to do it! He knows how to do everything!'

Charlotte swallowed back a very sour rejoinder. Fact was, Riccardo was fast moving into the stellar category of Superdad. He had also, unfairly, managed to deflect all negative press reporting by flinging his hands up in the air and *coming clean*. A youthful romance, a baby he had known nothing about, a marriage proposed and turned down, responsibilities accepted, *welcomed*. He was the man willing to turn his whole life upside down for the sake of his daughter, but for reasons beyond his comprehension Charlotte had rejected his pleas to formalise their relationship. He made a lot of heart-warming references to old-fashioned values, respect for family life, and in short managed to make her seem not just ridiculously stupid, for turning down a marriage proposal from a man who could click his fingers and have any woman he wanted, but also selfish, cold and proud to the point of lunacy.

In the face of these implications, Charlotte kept resolutely silent, fearing that one slipped word would be embroidered into God only knew what.

But the past few days had been hellish, and the lurking men at the gate outside was proving to be the final straw.

She grabbed Gina and hurtled outside, wearing an expression that could curdle milk. She met the same old questions, this time more intrusive, as one of them snidely implied that she might be positioning herself for a custody battle considering she was prepared to put her welfare above that of her daughter's.

Charlotte picked up her pace but she was perspiring by the time she was safely inside her car, windows rolled up against the clatter of voices outside.

On the way to school, she heard herself chatting to Gina, asking all the usual questions about homework, and making sure she ate all of her lunch. In her head, she replayed what that damned reporter had said about the possibility of a custody fight.

Could that happen? She feverishly wondered where he had managed to pluck that random statement from. Had Riccardo said anything about a custody battle? He had said nothing to *her*, had been decent and sympathetic about the whole press-invasion business, but had he let slip some intention to the wrong ears?

Whilst driving to the school and dropping Gina off, the seeds of unease had blossomed into full-blown panic, and she called in to the office, for the first time ever, with a phoney excuse about getting in late because of a blinding headache.

The slightest mention of Riccardo and they would be buzzing with curiosity. Honestly, it wasn't as though her circumstances had changed! She was still a hard-working mum with an eight-year-old daughter. How could scandal have wrapped itself around her so completely when, *technically* speaking, things were pretty much the same, give or take the sudden appearance of a wealthy Italian? Admittedly with looks to die for and a surprising flair for the role of martyr…

She got through to Riccardo on the second ring and didn't bother with pleasantries.

'I need to see you right now.'

Riccardo had programmed her into his mobile phone. He knew, as soon as his phone buzzed, that she would be on the other end of the line. He also knew what she wanted to see him about.

'Right now. Interesting that you think you can just pop in whenever it suits you.' He swivelled his chair so that he was facing the window. Moving out had been an error of judgement. His apartment seemed too big and too empty for just one. Having spent a lifetime without the slightest flicker of paternal yearnings to disturb the calm, ordered and preordained course of his formidably disciplined life, he had discovered that he missed his daughter, missed watching her as she sat frowning in front of her homework, missed the silly questions apropos of nothing in particular, missed the board games which had become a long-distant memory from his own childhood.

He also missed *her*—Charlotte. After a stressful day at work, when before he had looked to his blonde, leggy bimbos to distract him with the game of flirtation and sex, he had found himself looking forward to the peace and relaxation of her company, to her quick sense of humour, and that reluctant smile that lit up her face when he'd said something she couldn't help but find amusing.

Never one to sit around brooding over emotional dilemmas, Riccardo had decided that he would not accept what he had increasingly found to be the unacceptable. He would not accept the visiting rights to his daughter, with the so-called benefits of being able to return to his former life of pointless women and meals out. Half a life was not better than no life at all. Half a life was, for him, just a challenge, and he had risen to the challenge with the same brutal precision that had seen him climb over the years to the top of the jungle.

'This is all your fault, Riccardo,' Charlotte said, not bothering to wrap up the accusation in any phoney packaging.

'So what's new?'

'I'm not going to get into an argument with you on the telephone,' Charlotte snapped. 'I'm on my way to the underground.'

'When are you ever going to listen to me and *take taxis* when you want to get around?'

'Oh, for goodness' sake, Riccardo!' Momentarily distracted, Charlotte clicked her tongue in annoyance and stifled the little spurt of pleasure his words generated. Belatedly, she remembered that this was what Italian men were all about. Give Riccardo an available blonde, and he was all passion and fire. Give him the mother of his child, and he became solicitous and weirdly old-fashioned. Hence that pious, moral stance that had resulted in her having all the negative press chucked at her front door. Which fired her up all over again.

'I'll be at your office in forty minutes or so. Now, are you going to see me or aren't you? Because I want to talk to you, and if you don't see me I shall just sit in front of your office until you do.'

Now *that*, Riccardo thought, would really cause a stir—the mother of his child camping out at his office door! The wagging tongues, which feared him too much to wag in front of him, would be in full force.

'I'll meet you in the boardroom suite on the top floor

in precisely forty-five minutes. Take the executive lift up. I'll make sure the people on Reception know that you're expected.'

Charlotte had very little doubt that they would have denied her entry, when her face had been splashed all over the gossip columns like a criminal in a 'wanted' ad.

She made it to Riccardo's office in record time and headed for the lift to the boardroom suite with her head down, not wanting to catch anyone's eye, and resenting that she was forced into hiding because of a situation over which she had had no control.

The boardroom was literally a suite. One vast room was dominated by a long walnut table with sufficient seating for twenty. Spanning out from that central space was a luxury bathroom, which perplexed Charlotte as she took advantage of arriving twenty minutes early to snoop around. What executive would suddenly find himself in need of a quick shower before the next high-level conference? Then there was a library stocked with shelves of books, the titles of which were sufficient to induce sudden sleepiness, and a table on which was fanned out every national newspaper. Including, she noticed wryly, the ones best known for their salacious girlie pictures. Finally, there was a big sitting area, decked out in soft sofas and chairs, and along one wall all the facilities needed to make drinks of both an alcoholic and non-alcoholic nature.

Charlotte took up position on one of the pale blue comfy chairs facing the door and leant forward, hands clasped over one crossed knee.

As always, the impact of seeing him momentarily

took her breath away as he entered the room, one hand tucked elegantly into his trouser pocket. It was still early. The tie was still on. Usually, when he'd returned to the house in the early evenings, the tie would have been off, the top two buttons of his shirt undone, as though restlessness had got the better of him during the course of the day.

She winced at the unwelcome reminder of what it had been like to share a house with him.

'How could you?' she demanded bluntly, watching as he sauntered over to a chair and book up position facing her. Charlotte stood up, walked across to the table groaning under the weight of newspapers, and picked up one of the tabloids, opening it to the centre pages and dumping it on his lap so that he could see the headlines in all their glory—TYCOON'S LOVE-CHILD IN TUG OF WAR!

Riccardo glanced down at it with disinterest. 'You should never read the gossip columns, Charlie. I never do.'

'Well, bully for you, Riccardo!' She planted herself in front of him, hands on her hips. 'I have no ivory towers to hide behind! I have to go out to work and take Gina to school, and there are *reporters swarming everywhere*!' Slight exaggeration, prompted by his cool-as-a-cucumber attitude. 'They're making life a living hell for us, Riccardo,' she continued, gratified to see that he at least seemed to be giving her words some consideration. 'They're asking questions, and even though I don't give them answers they're still jotting stuff down, so I'm in constant fear of what I'll read in the press!'

'How is Gina dealing with the attention?'

Seems fairly thrilled. 'Distraught.'

'She didn't seem too distraught when I spoke to her on the telephone last night.'

'She's hiding it well. She doesn't want to let you down.' She swept one hand through her hair and returned to flop down on the chair. 'Did you have to go and tell them all that stuff about proposing marriage and being turned down? You could have just kept a low profile and everything would have blown over by now. Instead, what do you do? Blather on about values and tradition, making me out to be selfish and heartless!'

'I did warn you that the press might get involved.'

'Yes, I know *that*! But did you have to be so...*long winded* with them?'

'I've found that it's the only way to get rid of them. The slightest hint of any cloak and dagger stuff and they immediately think that there's something to hide. Give them the barest bones and then walk away.'

'I wouldn't call your marriage proposal the "barest bones". Actually, I think that would come under the heading of some pretty meaty stuff,' Charlotte said waspishly.

'Have you had any breakfast?'

'How can I eat?' She glared at him. 'My stomach's a mess.'

'I'll get them to bring you up something. Scrambled eggs on toast all right?'

It sounded yummy to Charlotte. 'I'm not hungry. I've completely lost my appetite with all that's been going on.'

'Mmm. Yes. Believe me, I do understand.' For a woman with no appetite and nerves that were shredded, she still managed to look damned sexy in that little pinstriped number. '*I* was a little taken aback when I first found my face in the Italian nationals for something trivial.'

'I'm more than a little *taken aback*, Riccardo.'

'I'd get them off your case if I could, but...' He shrugged elegantly and rose to his feet to get them both a cup of coffee. His secretary had seen fit to brew some fresh when she'd known that he required use of the top floor. He was back within minutes, carrying two cups of steaming coffee and a plate of biscuits which Charlotte briefly considered ignoring, before giving in to hunger. The truth was she really hadn't eaten any breakfast. The reporters by the gate had unnerved her, and besides Gina's costume had been patched together virtually at the eleventh hour. She had still been sewing on buttons when Gina had sat down for her bowl of cereal.

'But *what*? If you wanted to, you could...could tell them to back off.'

'They're having a field day at the moment with this,' Riccardo drawled, stretching out his legs and sipping from the china cup which looked inappropriate in his big hands. 'The world's a grim place, and in a grim place there's nothing like some juicy gossip to lighten the atmosphere.'

'I don't like the atmosphere being lightened at my expense.'

'Nor do I.' Riccardo watched her flustered face over the rim of his cup. Had she really thought that he would be able to turn off the media attention the way he could turn off a tap? He felt himself puff up like a horny teenager being given a sideways glance by the hot girl in the class. 'Spare a thought for me,' he continued, and was amused to see from her expression that the last thing she felt inclined to do was spare a thought for him. 'My reputation has been put through the wringer.'

'Riccardo, you didn't *have* a reputation. Well, you did—a reputation for being successful in your field and going out with empty-headed blondes like the one I met.'

'Now if you came here to insult me…'

'I didn't,' Charlotte said hurriedly. She sighed. 'Okay. You're more used to this sort of thing. How long can I expect it to last? It's wearing me down.'

This will be someone's fish-and-chip wrapping by the end of the week, Riccardo thought. 'Who can predict the appetite of gossip mongers? And who knows how far they'll dig?'

'How far they'll dig?' Charlotte said weakly.

'Look…' Riccardo leaned forward, resting his elbows on his knees and thoughtfully rubbing his thumbs together. 'It's always ugly when the press get hold of someone's personal life. There's a reason they're called mud-rakers. Now, it really doesn't affect me, but, yes, I am concerned for Gina. She's distraught, as you have told me.'

Charlotte uneasily wondered whether that little exaggeration had been such a good idea. 'Well…perhaps "distraught" is a bit overblown.'

'Okay, then. *Distressed.*'

'Yes, well…'

'I know you might not care for this alternative…' Riccardo lowered his voice, a man giving great thought and consideration to a delicate issue. 'But I can protect Gina more if she's with me.'

'No!'

'Hear me out, Charlie!' The lazy voice was suddenly as sharp as the crack of a whip, and Charlotte sat up, momentarily lost for speech. 'The reporters that swarm around you wouldn't dare do the same with me. I have people who fend my calls, and when my line is temporarily redirected, as it is now, they simply siphon off the unwelcomed calls. If someone I know needs to talk to me, they have my mobile number. I also have bodyguards. You wouldn't have noticed them. They're very discreet, and of course will disappear if I ask them to.'

'You have *bodyguards*? What kind of world do you live in?'

'The kind of world where the wealthy are possible targets. You forget, I am Italian. My country has its own past history of kidnappings. If Gina were with me, I could ensure that at least some of the inconveniences of what she is experiencing now could be dealt with.'

'No way!' Charlotte was still recovering from the shock of knowing that Riccardo had *bodyguards*. Where had they been lurking when he had been staying with her? Behind the bushes in the back garden? Under the mat at the front door? She worried at the idea now put into her head that, with all the publicity going on like a whirlpool around them—from which she was emerging in a pretty poor light through no fault of her own—Riccardo would stand a fair chance of persuading a court of law that, decent and honourable man that he was, he might be more suitable as a full-time carer. Even though he had given no hint that he might have that trick up his sleeve. Even though logic and reason told her that judge would probably file in favour of the mother. But doubts, even unreasonable doubts, had a nasty habit of creeping under the skin like a deadly virus.

'*Why* no way?' Riccardo asked in a long-suffering voice. 'We both want what's best for her, don't we?'

'Yes, well, she's coping all right at the moment.'

'I thought you said that she wasn't.'

'It's a nuisance.'

'And you came here to put the blame firmly at my door,' Riccardo said dryly.

'No!' Charlotte flushed uncomfortably.

'You saw a couple of reporters and blew a fuse. Look, there's another solution to this problem, and maybe this time you'll give it a bit more thought. Neither of us wants to be in the glaring limelight. You have a job to do, as do I, and Gina has to go to school without her life being disrupted. We continue as we are and who knows how long we'll be a scandalous affair.'

Charlotte snorted sourly under her breath. 'None of this would have happened if you weren't such a big cheese.'

Riccardo raised his eyebrows and smiled slowly at her, and Charlotte reluctantly grinned back.

'Marry me,' he said abruptly, never imagining he would return to this place having once been rejected. He noticed that she didn't immediately recoil. 'As a couple, we would have no story. A normal life, Charlie. You could keep your job, even though it's not in my nature to see my wife work, and you wouldn't have to think that at any given time you might be pounced on by a reporter wanting an update. You've seen how the kids of wealthy people can become specimens under the tabloid press microscopes…'

'Not *all*.' So, he hadn't mentioned the 'L' word, so she still had all her arguments about marriages of convenience being empty shells—but she had lived with him...shared the same space. She had liked it, whether she was willing to admit it or not, had liked seeing her daughter with her father. In life, people made sacrifices. She would sacrifice the perfect dream and instead live out the shared one, one in which she loved but was not loved in return. She'd be liked, though, and as the mother of his child always respected. Would it really be so bad?

And no more hassle with *anyone*. The curious looks at work would come to an end, as would the nagging suspicion that she might be recognised by perfect strangers because they could place her face from somewhere. Normal had never looked so good.

'And, like you say, all this will blow over in time...' She imagined being able to rely on someone else in a way she had never been able to in her life before. Someone who could share her concerns when Gina was ill, or had difficult homework. Someone who could help with the big decisions in her daughter's life, the schools she would attend. The list of temptations grew steadily longer.

'Also,' Riccardo said silkily. 'Look at it from my point of view for a minute instead of your own: I want to be able to give Gina all the things money can buy.'

'Which is the wrong way to bring up a child!' Charlotte said robustly.

Riccardo didn't miss a beat. He could sense her coming round, and the nearer he got to his goal the more he wanted it. 'Which is why I shall rely on you to rein me in when I want to show up at the house with a ten-foot pink elephant or the latest-model quad bike.'

Charlotte shuddered, and in the intervening silence Riccardo steamrollered on, not giving her time to backtrack over the old arguments against which he had no adequate responses. 'Better that than for Gina to grow up and witness the disparity in our lifestyles.'

'Meaning that you would be able to tempt her away from me just because you could lavish her with whatever she wanted?' But he had hit an open nerve, because she knew that with the best will in the world children could be swayed. The latest-model quad bike would always look better and shinier than the home-made doll's house under the Christmas tree. It wasn't fair and it wasn't right, but it was life. And, even if Gina held firm and was sensible enough to make the right judgements, how fair would it be that she should have to be put through the process of choice simply because her mother didn't want to marry Riccardo because he didn't love her the way she loved him?

'I would never, ever set out to do any such thing…'

The 'but' hung in the air between them like a sharpened knife ready to drop.

'Will you give me time to consider it?'

Riccardo knew that the deal was done. 'We couldn't continue to live in your house,' he said briskly, making sure that she didn't see his pleasure. 'It is too small for the three of us.'

'We managed just—'

'Which in turn might mean taking Gina out of her school, transferring her to another.'

'She's happy there, and she's not moving.'

Riccardo decided, in the interests of peace-making, not to pursue the point. 'Fine. But we move, and who better to source the right place than you?'

'I haven't yet made my mind up,' Charlotte said weakly.

'You have. Now all we need to do is sort out the details.'

Step one in growing up had been having Gina. Now, step two was the realisation that nothing really worked out the way you truly wanted. But he was right, and there was no use pretending. Her mind *was* made up bar the shouting, and, yes, the details would have to be worked out.

'We'll have to tell Gina.' She lowered her eyes because she could feel the glitter of tears brightening them.

'This evening,' Riccardo agreed. 'And, whilst you can source locations and possibilities, I would want the three of us to look at any potential houses together.'

'I don't know what kind of house you would want.' Things seemed to be moving at breakneck speed, and she tried to yank it back to a pace she could deal with.

'You know me. You know the kind of place I'd be comfortable with.'

'I *don't* know you.'

'Of course you do. You know me better than any other woman has ever done.' Riccardo shocked himself with the admission. A whisper of vulnerability threaded its way through his body and he fought it away. 'I know you probably have ideas on weddings. All women seem to. I am happy to go along with whatever you want. Big, small, fancy, simple…'

'I don't care.'

Riccardo watched her downbent face with narrowed eyes, feeling like the executioner dragging someone to the guillotine. Was this how she truly saw him? Still? Was she coming to him defeated, because he had cleverly put her in a position from which she saw no retreat? Dammit, he was trying!

'Your call. But I won't sit around waiting. If you don't care, then you won't mind getting married quietly in the Register Office at Marylebone.'

Charlotte shrugged. Gina would be over the moon, which was a cheerful thought. 'What do we do about…?'

'About what?'

'About…'

Comprehension dawned, and Riccardo gave her a slow, wolfish smile. 'Sleeping arrangements? To put it delicately.'

'You slept in the guest room before.'

'That was then and this is now,' Riccardo drawled. 'When I am your husband, then I have no intention of our marriage being in name only. And there's no need to look so primly offended at the prospect.'

He pushed himself out of the chair and strolled over to Charlotte, so that he could lean over her, hands on either side of her chair. 'We both know that when all the talk of our union being for convenience only is over, there is still left the interesting fact that we want one another. Look at you. Eyes as wide as saucers, pupils dilated.' He lifted one hand and tugged her bottom lip gently with his finger. It was all the more erotic because his eyes remained pinned to her face. 'Wouldn't you like me to touch you right here? Right now?'

'No, I would *not*!' What should have been a firm, controlled, maybe even slightly amused protest—because spinsterish outrage had just not been cutting it—emerged as a strangulated gasp for air, with a feeble denial thrown in for good measure.

'Tut, tut, Charlie. You'll really have to do a bit better than that…' He leant into her and covered her mouth with his, sliding his tongue between her lips, which were parted in surprise.

In that split second, Charlotte realised that she was no longer going to fight him. She loved him and she would take what she could, because her previous efforts at self-denial had been painful and futile. Her body melted and she arched up to return his kiss, feeding his hunger with her own. She felt his momentary surprise, and wondered whether he had been expecting her to put up her usual resistance, but then it was as if her response had fired up something in him, something savage and urgent. He pulled her to her feet, backing her slowly but inexorably towards the cool wall until she was pressed back against it.

They managed to remove her jacket without breaking apart, and she helped him as he began unbuttoning her blouse until he could reach inside and caress her aching, tender breasts through the lacy bra.

Riccardo was dimly aware of the inappropriate nature of their surroundings. He was breaking every single one of his own codes of practice by doing what he was doing in the sanctum of his working environment. Women had always been for pleasure, and pleasure had never crossed over into his working life. The two had been kept apart, physically and mentally.

But he couldn't help himself. Not when her breasts were pushing against that bra, begging to be suckled. He ground his body against her, letting her know how aroused he was, and he almost embarrassed himself by ejaculating as she rubbed him through his trousers.

His secretary would know better than to disturb him when she knew he was using the top floor. They would not be interrupted, and right now he had to have her, needed to taste every inch of her body, from her nipples all the way down to the honeyed moisture between her legs. His body was on fire and starving, and common sense would just have to wait.

CHAPTER TEN

BUMPING into Ben three days later was an accident of chance, and in the interim Charlotte had had ample time to wonder what she had got herself into. An emotional quagmire, or so it seemed, in which the main protagonists, Gina and Riccardo, were very happy, leaving her to nurse her confusion on her own. In her head.

Both she and Riccardo had spoken to Gina together. They had anticipated questions, but Gina had accepted this new, startling change of events with an ingenuous lack of curiosity. Typical eight-year-old. Precociously bright she might be, but when it had come to Mummy and Daddy getting married there had been nothing incisive about her exclaiming 'Great! Can my friends come round and meet my dad?'

And the press, alerted by invisible radar, had changed from pursuit to writing treacly praise for the importance of marriage. Within this framework, Riccardo seemed very satisfied because he had, she acknowledged, got precisely what he had wanted from the very first minute he'd realised that he had a daughter. And he even had *her* thrown in for good measure.

He had all but moved in, and when he'd been around his eyes had followed her, he'd made sure to touch her, even in passing, and when Gina hadn't been around he'd pinned her against the wall and they had stolen their heated kisses like star-crossed lovers. And that was the one thing they weren't, because 'love' was the taboo word that had been resoundingly absent in all his dealings with her. He was content with the lust, and she no longer had the strength or the conviction to resist it.

She had resigned herself to the unhappy prospect of wondering when the lust would end and when he would begin to discreetly cast his net further afield in search of more nubile pastures. She would probably never know, because he would leave no careless signs behind him, and he would continue to treat her with the respect due to her position in his life. And she would never confront him, because she knew already that ignorance would be bliss.

Ben was lucky enough to find her at midday on a sullen, overcast Thursday, sitting in her office with an untouched sandwich next to her, supposedly mulling over a report on first-time buyers and interest rates, but instead gloomily contemplating her life.

It was a few seconds before Charlotte was even aware of his presence by her door, and a few more seconds before she registered who he was, but when she did she found that she was overjoyed to see him. She had spoken to him a couple of times after the story had broken, and he was the only one she had been honest with, and the only one who had not given her a hearty little pep-talk on how lucky she was to have landed the biggest fish in the sea.

'That's not a good look for someone living out the fairy-tale dream,' was the first thing he said as he stepped into the office and shut the door behind him. 'What's wrong, Charlotte?'

'*What's wrong?* How much time have you got to spare?' She gave a manic little laugh that ended on a strangled sob.

'Okay, my girl. On your feet. I'm taking you out to lunch.'

'I can't, Ben. I've got *all this*.' She waved her hand to take in the computer and the stacks of paperwork sitting on her desk, patiently waiting for her to get her act together.

'You still have to eat. Now, up. We won't go far. I'll have you safely delivered back to the grindstone by one. I'm here for a meeting with Parry at one-thirty, anyway.'

'Honestly, Ben, don't ruin your plans for me. I know you just popped in to say hi.' She stood up. 'But I'm not getting any work done, and lunch out is just what I need. I can't tell you how miserable it is being the luckiest girl in the world.'

They went to a brasserie round the corner from the office. They could be guaranteed a certain amount of privacy there, because the food was delicious but wildly overpriced and everyone else in the office avoided the place like the plague. It was also the perfect place to have an emotional conversation without risk of being overheard. The tables were helpfully spaced apart and the atmosphere, even at midday, was curiously intimate.

Without too much prompting, Charlotte poured out her heart. Ben provided the handkerchief, and over an expensive, exquisite beefburger listened to her rambling tale of love and panic, and confusion and love, and lust and uncertainty, and more love. He remained stoic when she told him with an anguished groan that she wished to God she could have loved *him* the way she loved Riccardo. Ben, who had just started seeing another woman, hoped for the adoration Charlotte obviously still felt for her ex-boyfriend and now husband-to-be. To have that would be nice. Standing outside, he was pleased to see that Charlotte looked a lot less teary, even though he had offered no helpful pieces of advice but had just listened. When she hugged him, he freely wrapped her in his arms and gave her a brotherly kiss on her forehead.

Across the road, Riccardo was halted in his tracks. He hadn't expected this. The girl at the office had told him that Charlotte had gone to lunch at that expensive place round the corner; she couldn't remember the name but it was something French. She hadn't said anything about the man Charlotte had gone with, and Riccardo had assumed… What had he assumed? That she was tied to him in some way simply because she had finally given in to her physical attraction? Hadn't she told him often enough that lust was not the glue that held a relationship together? What the hell had he been thinking?

He watched from a distance as she stood still on the pavement for a few seconds on her own, wrapping her arms around herself. She was smiling, and from where he was standing that smile looked mighty happy indeed.

Riccardo felt the blood which had drained away from

his body rush to his head in a burst of jealous, possessive rage. He was shaking as he leant heavily against the wall and drew in one long, shuddering breath. Then he turned away and began walking. He didn't go near his office. Trying to work would have been impossible. For the first time since he had been living in London, he did the unthinkable and took a taxi to Regent's Park, which was peaceful and fairly deserted. In his head, he replayed what had confronted him outside the brasserie. His wife to be, his *woman*, wrapped up in the arms of another man. There was a heavy sensation in the pit of his stomach which felt like concrete.

He should have talked to her before, really talked. But how could he have, when he had known nothing of how he felt about her until an hour ago? When he had witnessed her in the arms of her ex-boyfriend. If indeed he *was* an 'ex'.

The prospect of living a life walking in the shadow of someone else filled him with searing rage and now he knew why. He dialled her number on his mobile phone without bothering to torture himself with self-analysis, and got through to her immediately.

'I need to see you,' he told her. 'Right now.'

'I've got a stack of work to do, Riccardo. Can it wait until later?' Having lunch with Ben had been a good idea. Charlotte felt calmer now, more resigned to her destiny. She couldn't resist Riccardo, and that being the case then she would have to stop acting as though the world had caved in. No one was more pitiful than the person who moped around feeling sorry for herself. She had made her choice and she would live with it and accept its limitations.

'No. Do you want me to meet you at your office?'

'No,' Charlotte said hurriedly, shuddering at the thought of every member of staff subjecting them to in-depth scrutiny. 'Where are you now?'

'Regent's Park.'

'You're in *Regent's Park*?'

'You can always come here, but it's a dreary day to be outside.'

'Okay. I'll meet you at the house. I can bring some of this work back with me and do it later after Gina's gone to bed. Is…is everything okay?'

'No. But I'll explain when I see you.'

It was so unlike Riccardo to say something like that that Charlotte felt a flutter of fear. She couldn't pack her things up fast enough, and on the Tube back her head was filled with sickening scenarios. Had he changed his mind about marrying her? Maybe her behaviour had finally turned him off. Maybe sleeping with a woman while suspecting she didn't like him had awakened in him the obvious desire to have more than just a body. She had lain in his arms and still kept him at a distance. She had been aware of doing that, and now she wondered whether he had finally got fed up with her sour grapes. He wasn't to know that she'd just been trying to protect herself.

Or maybe he was ill. That disturbing thought sneaked its way into her subconscious, and once there refused to go away. Why else would he have been at Regent's Park, of all places? If there was something seriously wrong with him, then what better place for peace, to think things through?

From these two scenarios, worrying offshoots wreaked havoc with her nervous system, and she was white-faced by the time she made it to the house and let herself in.

'I'm in here.'

Charlotte dropped her bag and briefcase and kicked off her shoes. She found him in the sitting room, lights off, nursing a cup of coffee. He looked at her, then back at the coffee, as if hoping to find inspiration in the mug, like a reader of tea leaves.

'What's wrong?' she demanded. 'Why were you sitting in Regent's Park at this time of day?'

'Sit down.' He watched as she scuttled across to the chair. Yes, she could melt in his arms, *had* melted in his arms, because she couldn't resist his touch, but what good was that when she still shied away from him like a scared rabbit whenever he wasn't touching her? He thought with regret of how she had wanted him all those years ago and how he had thrown it all away because his bright, glittering future had had no place for her at that time. Now, ensconced in his bright, glittering future, he could only think how much he wanted that girl back, the one who curved willingly into his arms and would never have sat watching him cautiously from the furthest possible chair, her body language stiff with tension.

'I came to your office today.' He stood up abruptly, wishing to God he had had the sense to have poured himself something a little stronger than a cup of coffee.

'You did? When? I didn't see you.'

'I was told that you had gone out for lunch.'

'Oh, right. Yes.' Charlotte thought uncomfortably about Ben and reddened.

Watching her, Riccardo now knew for sure that she still had an ongoing relationship with the other man. So maybe she wasn't sleeping with him, but she was giving him her love, and what greater gift was there, after all?

'How long has it been going on?' he asked roughly, pushing himself to his feet and pacing the room.

Charlotte wearily wondered whether she was letting herself back in for another speech about relinquishing all contact with every other man on the face of the earth, even if the contact was perfectly innocent, because that was the *Italian* way. Never mind that he wouldn't have a problem with his *Italian* way allowing him to take a mistress as and when he so desired.

She opened her mouth to speak, but he silenced her with his hand. 'No. Don't answer that. I don't have a right to know and I do not want to, anyway.'

'You mean you're not going to lay down laws about Ben? I don't believe you!' She laughed, but nervously, because this too was unlike the Riccardo she knew. Which brought her right back to the 'seriously ill' theory.

'I gave you up eight years ago, Charlie. I have no right to ask anything of you now.' He dragged a chair closer to hers and sat down heavily, raking his fingers through his hair before resting his arms loosely on his thighs.

'But I want to.'

'Want to *what*?'

'Ask a millions things of you. Ask you not to see that man ever again. Ask you never to even let him cross your *mind*. I have a problem with him. I have a problem with your friendship with him.'

'You mean you're *jealous*?' Charlotte asked incredulously, and Riccardo flushed.

'What's so weird about that?' he asked, his head snapping up. 'I am a jealous man. Of course I can't bear the thought of you enjoying the company of another man.'

'But Ben isn't *competition*.'

'No. Because you have reluctantly come round to my proposal and decided to marry me.' His eyes tangled with hers and Charlotte felt her heart do a crazy loop. She wanted to tell him to spend a little more time discussing the jealousy issue, because just the thought of that sent an illicit thrill racing through her. 'But I see now that you were right all along. Reluctant acceptance…a business arrangement, call it what you will…just is not good enough. For either of us. I thought that it would be fine, that it was in the best interests of our daughter, but now…'

'Now you've changed your mind.'

Riccardo nodded with difficulty and tried to marshal his thoughts. 'We were happy once.' *No.* Just referring to their happiness in the past tense scared him because it made him realise that it might be lost to him for ever and there would be nothing he could do about it. Money could buy him anything on the face of the earth, but if she turned him away then nothing it could buy would be of any value. 'I know what you think of me. But we could be happy again. I…was happy when we were living together, and if I didn't show it then that was my fault. Don't say anything. I just want you to think about what I am going to say to you, and if you still don't want me then so be it.'

Charlotte didn't think there was anything she *could* say, because her tongue seemed to be glued to the roof of her mouth.

'Eight years ago, I let you go. We were both too young, and there was too much living left to do to settle down with one person.'

'I know.' Her cheeks were tinged with dull colour. 'We've gone over this ground a million times before. I thought we'd made peace with the past.'

'What I am trying to say is that the best thing that ever happened in my life was the day you walked back into it.' His dark eyes met hers, and Charlotte held her breath, not wanting to shatter the moment. 'Yes, I was furious that you had had a child, *my* child, and not seen fit to tell me. But when I saw you again…' He relived the moment and briefly closed his eyes before looking at her. 'Everything that had once been there flooded back. It was as though those eight years of absence had never been.'

'What do you mean?' Charlotte was almost too afraid to ask just in case she had missed some very obvious agenda that would put paid to the soaring hope blossoming inside her.

'For eight years I did what I was programmed to do,' Riccardo said heavily. 'And I enjoyed it, or I thought I did. Women came and went, and I figured that was perfectly normal.' He glanced down at his fingers and thought how odd it felt to be at the mercy of something he couldn't rationalise. 'You came along, Charlie, and it was as though I had been living half a life. I don't want to marry you just for the sake of Gina. I want to marry you for *me*, because I can't go back to that half life. And, before you say a word, I can make you happy.'

He went over to her and sat on the arm of her chair because somehow, by being physically close, she might absorb the urgency of what he was saying. 'You think you need the safety of that other man, but you don't. All I am asking is a chance… I love you, my darling. You complete me.'

'Perhaps you could say that again?' Charlotte at last found her voice and she smiled at him, a wide, blissful smile that lit up her face.

'Come on, Charlie,' Riccardo, watching the transformation of her expression, felt deliriously happy. 'I've bared my soul. Now it's your turn.'

Neither was allowed to let the grass grow under their feet. Gina made sure of that. She wanted to be a part of everything, and no decision was to be made without her consultation. The dreaded meeting with Riccardo's mother turned out to be not quite the terrible event Charlotte had envisaged.

'She'll hate me,' she'd told Riccardo, the day before his mother was due to land for a long weekend with them. 'She'll complain about the size of my house. She'll complain about *everything*.' She could remember all too well the austere, aristocratic bearing and the disparaging, soul-destroying personality. But Riccardo had been right to reassure her that his mother had mellowed over time, and Gina had broken the ice. The two together had formed an amusing and conspirational relationship which oversaw the details of the wedding, and six months later, Charlotte and Riccardo had been married. It was a fairly small service, followed by a much bigger reception, and afterwards a fortnight in Italy, during which they'd barely seen their daughter who'd done the rounds of relatives and had been overjoyed to be the centre of attention.

Riccardo, who increasingly found it hard to understand how he could have lived his life without Charlotte, returned to their new, spacious house in Richmond every evening to the warmth of his family. And when, on their first anniversary, he was informed that he was going to be a father for the second time, he felt pride and joy swell inside his heart for the woman sitting opposite him in the restaurant, demurely sipping from her glass of mineral water.

'You'll give up work, won't you?' She had stayed on to oversee the running of the office on a part-time basis, and now she nodded, with a slow smile.

'Can't wait. Gina's settled in her new school, life is settled…' She could feel tears of happiness well up. 'And it's about time you did it the Italian way and started supporting me!' Then she grinned, because it was only what he had wanted from the minute she had looked at him and said, 'I do…'

THE MILE-HIGH CLUB

by Heidi Rice

Celebrity Jack Devlin had shared a night of passion with magazine assistant Mel. Now the dark, brooding millionaire had asked her to write the exclusive story on his life. Travelling first class, she would join the jet set (and the mile-high club!) in spectacular style...but only for a week or two. For it seemed Jack would never trust anyone enough to offer more than an intensely passionate affair...

BEDDED BY ARRANGEMENT

by Natalie Anderson

Jake Rendel is a millionaire who works hard and plays hard – unlike his old neighbour, Emma Delaney, who is stifled by her uninspiring job. So whilst Jake's in town he makes Emma an offer to shake off her prim and proper image: for a month they'll pretend to be having a hot and steamy affair! Emma's out of her depth – and all too soon this girl-next-door is wishing the month will never end...

...International affairs, seduction and passion guaranteed

VOLUME FIVE

Expecting His Royal Baby by Susan Stephens

Nico Fierezza: as an internationally successful magnate, he's never needed to rely on his family's royal name. But now he's back – and the King has matched him with a suitable bride. Niroli is ready to welcome its new ruler!

Carrie Evans has been in love with Nico, her boss, for years. But, after one magical night of loving, he ruthlessly discarded her…and now she's discovered she's carrying his child!

Everything is in place for Nico's forthcoming nuptials. But there's an unexpected wedding guest: Carrie, who is willing to do anything to protect the future of her baby… The question is – does anything include marrying Nico?

Available 2nd November 2007